GOLLY SPRINGS

A novel by

Michael Frederick

Books by author:

White Shoulders

Places

Ledges

Blue River

The Paper Man

Different

Missouri Madness

Zed

Shy Ann

Drop 50 & Magnify

Summer of '02

Autumn Letters

Stuck

Indie Writer

King of Slugs

Already Bad/Volume 1

Already Bad/Volume 2

October, 2015/1st printing/2000 copies
Copyright 2015
all rights reserved

Thanks again, Tony, for your art.
Cover Design by Anthony Conrad

Ship of Fools

Imagine a healthy man of 19, born and raised in Dublin, crossing the Irish Sea on a coal ship in March of 1847. His goal: Virginia in America. He desperately wanted to escape the poverty and hunger that sails with him. This was an awful period for Ireland and England, a breeding ground for typhus and dysentery that was exacerbated by the poorest sanitation. This deadly combination was caused by the huddled masses living in squalor and human waste. One in five of Irish passengers stowed below deck sailing for Canada or America would end up with typhus, die, and be dumped overboard at sea without ceremony.

There were hardly any doctors to examine all the passengers thoroughly; unless a passenger appeared deathly ill they'd be herded on board like animals, stowed below deck from 30 to 90 days in lice-infested holding areas until reaching their destination.

Everson Shay Golly was 19, fit as a fiddle, when he left Dublin on a free 3-hour human ballast ride on an empty coal ship to Liverpool, England. Nearly all of these poor masses had been evicted and forced to leave the Emerald Isle that could no longer sustain them. There was no money and no work to buy food, only plentiful lies containing hope that work, food, and money were waiting for them in a new world in the Americas. Shay Golly, Everson's father, had his son bind and sew three British silver sterling coins worth about 15 shillings into the waist lining

1

of his trousers so that the coins didn't jingle about. Obvious sounds of money on any person could get them killed by any one of these desperate people.

There was an obvious abundance of false hope that kept these poor souls alive; and Everson Golly had more hope in his heart than most men his age. *"And, you'll need every bit of your heart to survive such a voyage to Virginia,"* his father warned. Everson's freckled fair skin and copper-red hair was like so many of his fleeing countrymen—they all looked alike: wretched. By the time young Golly stepped onto a Liverpool dock, he had his plan to improve his chances surviving the deadly fever of typhus: He would stay away from the rat-infested lodging houses that many passengers would share for days while waiting to board the *"coffin ships"* that would carry them and their dreams across a vast sea…if they could survive typhus. And: he had saved enough shillings to take a merchant ship to the United States since rumors were still going around that England wanted to populate Canada, and was charging three times the fare to sail to the U.S. He reasoned that by going on a more expensive voyage, his odds making it there improved with a healthier class of passengers who could afford the fare to the U.S.

Everson tried to stay clear of the man-swarm crowding the Liverpool docks and lodging houses waiting for their ship to sail. Yet it was impossible to avoid them. It rained hard off and on for two days while he walked around Liverpool in order to keep his sea legs, a thing his father advised him to do in order to avoid the sick. He would sleep alone in a dry doorway of a hovel for brief periods; then on he'd walk until finally the dismal gray of Liverpool vanished on his third day. On that glorious day when the sun broke out, Everson landed a job for free fare as a deck seaman on a Dutch clipper ship named The Dutchman, a 180-

foot, square-rigged merchant ship designed for speed. With a crew of 40 men and 180 Irish men, women and children stowed below deck, The Dutchman set sail with 6 tons of gun powder and 3 more tons of British musketry destined for an armory in Norfolk, Virginia.

Strapping Everson was given the lowest of duties on the ship. At first he thought his work on the ship would save his life by affording him plenty of fresh air and mess privileges with sleeping quarters with the crew. However, his duties were to ration food and water to the passengers below deck and to maintain sanitation in this darkest of places where 180 souls languished in deplorable conditions that Everson had never seen the likes of before –even on the streets of Dublin.

From the moment he unlocked the hatch and first climbed down to the stifling darkness he called "*the hell hole*," he vowed to his stubborn Irish mind to only breathe through his mouth and never speak a word until he reached Virginia.

Each grueling day got worse than the day before for the deck seaman's senses; deplorable sights, sounds and smells bombarded his being until he was numbed to the brink of madness. Such deprivations and human suffering he hadn't witnessed up close until quite early in the voyage when mothers, then children and men of all ages became ill with the typhus fever. The sounds of sick and terrified children clumped together in poor sanitation combined with the absence of the sun's healing light, forced Everson to toil 18 hours every day hoisting in buckets of contaminated drinking water and hoisting out never-ending buckets of human feces. All done in the darkness of rotting flesh and growing numbers of fever-lit eyes burning into his sensitive heart every move he made. All of this was hard on a sensitive man.

3

It got so he could smell the water stored in barrels topside that were never cleaned properly. These were the 200-lb. oak barrels that once held vinegar, olive oil, and pickles from Greece. These near-empty containers would be left open on the ship's deck and become filled with days of Liverpool rain for the poor-paying Irish cargo that had already been fooled in so many ways before even leaving England. Whenever he would drop then climb down the rope ladder into this dark holding area of these sick and poor wretched people, he would ladle out their daily water ration knowing that this kind of contaminated water could very easily cause sickness and at the very least keep them from recovering their health.

It was after two long weeks at sea that increasing death came to the ship, whereupon one or two bodies every day or so had to be placed inside a bag made of hemp and hoisted out by a pulley rope like contaminated goods about to be dropped into the sea.

One such typhus death was a young mother with two children, a girl of 2 or 3 and a lad of 6 or 7 years, Everson thought. These children were clutching at their mother while he was hoisting her out of their reach toward the blue light of sky that was blinding the children. Everson, in his raging anguish, sobbing so violently over this horrific loss for the children — grew weaker and weaker pulling the rope that hoisted the woman higher and higher until his heart nearly burst and his vow of silence ended. His first words startled the kids to a wide-eyed spooked silence as their mother's body twirled back and forth high above them under the blue light: *"She's on way to her God's Heaven, children! Let her go now...back to her creator...where she can watch over you from above!"* It was only their pitiful pleadings he had stilled; and now their pathetic little faces watched him raise their mother closer to the blue light. Tears and sweat fell from his face, splashing through

4

shards of sunlight and onto the pale skin of these children holding onto each other as he managed with trembling strength to raise her to the man waiting topside.

Within a few moments she was but another splash in the ocean, *"Not even a drop* in *a bucket,"* Golly thought, exhausted as he was. He knew these children were in the throes of shock and grief now, and that now was no time to try and explain the plan he had for them as he examined their bare arms for the dreaded red spots of the deadly typhus that killed their mother. He found none, and considered that a miracle. Everson knelt and whispered his plan to the boy; words that the deck seaman wanted to remain a secret. The boy nodded that he understood. He pulled on the rope that signaled for the rope ladder to be dropped down to him. Now he would climb and again cry on his way topside, knowing he would pull the ladder up and leave behind these new orphans that he was now attached to.

The ship's captain was a stern taskmaster known for swift punishment for small infractions. One of his orders to Golly was to keep the scourge of typhus and dysentery contained below deck, and that if his crew became infected –he would chain any of them with the Irish cargo until landing in Virginia. So Everson scrubbed around a small area away from the others near the ladder drop and moved the children there. Discreetly he gave the children some of his good water from the captain's supply that he kept in a patched goatskin container tied around his waist.

In near total darkness he would go from one listless body to the other, filling their water cups and doling out their ration of bread and oats into a separate tin cup, all the while thinking how he didn't want to know the names of the two children who had lost their mother. And he could feel their little blue eyes watching him as if he alone was the only one on earth who could help them in this dark world of early death, deprivations, and too

5

little joy. For their sake he would break his vow of silence again and again so that he could be their ray of hope and survive this voyage to Virginia with him.

He had no intention of uttering a word to those children until their mother died. Her death had changed him from a nineteen-year-old self-serving survivor to a compassionate, giving man. From the instant he came out of that hole and into the salty spray of the dipping then rising bow, that first deep inhalation of sea air into his lungs was filled with Irish will and determination to make certain that those two children made it to Virginia.

Now, as he made his way below deck to the ship's kitchen he knew he could find a fresh piece of fruit before the crew grabbed the best of it. He felt renewed energy and strength in his legs. All because he had found a new motivation, a way to stop counting the torturous days that were leaving him a bit weaker each day. His mind was on getting them fresh air and fruit, and a better place to sleep that was away from the snoring man-swarm and stifling dead-breath air coming and going every moment in that rocking box of vomit and waste he alone would haul out of there every day at sunset when the body eliminations were mostly done until morning. This was another strict order from the captain; he did not want to breathe the stench permeating through the ship's hull to his cabin upon retiring.

Those little urchins were now two new reasons to survive this voyage. Now The Dutchman's God-forsaken voyage had figuratively changed its course for Everson Golly, a new direction of spirit that was pleasing to his mind and body. He caught himself laughing at those Liverpool jackals, those ignorant dolts that made up the crew, men who just hours before, he ignored as bleary and grim reminders of things to be tolerated until his feet were on land again.

6

Now: these men of stained red faces made from sun and wind and rum would pass beside him along a narrow passageway, and he would look straight into their rheumy eyes and see a flashing of the storms they had weathered. Before, he had always looked down submissively because he could smell the meat swallowed on their hot breath mixed with the sweat-stained stench of their bodies. They all joked about the foolish Irish lad who had the worst duty on The Dutchman. Now: they were startled by his confident blue gaze that had new purpose and energy. As he shopped for fresh fruit he could see the blazing/dead eyes of their mother who never spoke a word to him; but now he was certain that her eyes were begging him to look after her children. Yes, he was now more certain than ever that he had seen that in her eyes when but days ago she had to know she was dying.

Those sage words of his father kept coming to his mind more now than ever: "*It's a one-way journey to America. Nobody I know has ever returned. So make America your home in your heart from now on. That way, Ever, you won't fall victim to self-doubt about leaving.*" "Ever" was the name his father called him; and that would be the name the children would come to know on his next visit to the hell hole.

Buck and Dolly

If the captain caught wind of what his deck seaman was doing on his ship with those two Irish runts, exposing his crew to the louse-borne "famine fever"—twenty lashes with a whip soaked in turpentine would be his punishment at the very least. Buck and Dolly were their names, two parts of a trio that had nine days of secrecy. Today Everson heard from the ship's helmsman that Virginia was ten days away if they could maintain their present speed. He told the kids to call him "Ever" and they did; instantly it became their new favorite name on this vessel delivering them to the New World.

On day 10 of their clandestine "routine" Ever had Buck hold a candle while he swabbed as close as possible to the infirm passengers that were too sick to move. So far they were lucky. Two hours before sunrise, when Ever was certain the crew was asleep he'd wake up from his private sleeping spot on the aft deck. Concealed by a hollowed out bowl that held ropes and slabs of cork used for emergency flotation, his bed was a half-score of empty hemp bags secured from the galley's consumed coffee, tea, and rice. Upon waking, in the rocking blackness of a moonless night, his bleary eyes would first inspect his arms and chest for the dreaded red spots. He would then go into hell and get the children, inspect them, and return with them to his sleeping area. He would feed them fresh fruit and nuts with the captain's good water.

They would nap on deck on the hemp bed, breathing in the sea's balmy air; then they'd be escorted back down into the hell hole before anyone was awake. This routine gave the kids an edge over the others, who seemed to be getting weaker by the day to Ever. Ever forbade his stowaways to speak while topside, so their keening voices were not heard by the lookout, who Ever knew to be a heavy sleeper by the sound of his blubbery-lipped snoring until ship's bells at sunrise. This risk was worth it to Ever, for now he was attached to them more than ever and needed them for his own well-being.

Ever had no siblings at home in Ireland. His mother died giving life to him. His father was a good man who worked every day of his life, and was a temperate drinker, so his only child was guided by this positive paternal presence his entire life. Because of his upbringing he wanted the same kind of life for Buck and Dolly, whose father had sailed to America and was never heard from again. This was when Dolly was un-born, and young Buck was told by his mother that they would find his father one day in America, and that is why they set sail on The Dutchman. When Ever asked Buck where his father was supposed to be landing in America, Buck answered with certainty, "*Virginia.*"

"Would you recognize your father if you saw him?" he whispered to the lad while Dolly slept in their secret place topside at the back of the ship. Buck nodded yes and proceeded to open a bundled piece of embroidered gold and red linen that held all their worldly possessions, something his mother had given him just days before she passed. His little fingers then opened another piece of lace cloth that covered an egg-sized oval frame with an encased wedding photo of Buck and Dolly's parents. "A handsome couple they were," Ever smiled with his

9

whisper. "And your father's name?" Ever was curious while staring into the moonlit photo.

"Lindell Dunn," Buck whispered proudly.

"What did your father do for work?"

The lad didn't know.

"Did your father send for you?"

Another negative nod, yet without any sense of loss or resignation on Buck's face.

Whenever they napped in their hiding place Ever was always the last to fall asleep. He would sleep with his bare back to the children while his gray and tattered work shirt was left hanging nearby to be mist-cleaned and air-dried by sea breezes that blew constantly. Compared to himself the children were malodorous and he wished every day he had some way of sneaking them into the galley where he could bath them with the same hot water and soap the officers were afforded before their breakfast.

On this particular pre-dawn he awoke earlier from his nap and went below deck to the galley to haul back a bucket of hot water along with a cake of soap he had hidden days ago in case this moment arrived. Before nodding off to sleep last night he had found his excuse if he was caught with the water; he would say it was for himself since he wanted to clean himself before cleaning the captain's quarters. Since the crew was aware how particular their captain was regarding his personal hygiene –not a man would dare challenge the deck seaman who swabbed the quarantined hell hole where typhus and dysentery lived.

Unseen in the dark passageways he knew from memory, he filled a bucket halfway with tepid water and placed it on the iron grate above the dying coal embers left from the evening meal. Upon retrieving the hidden cake of soap he waited for what seemed an eternity in the rocking galley that made foreboding sounds of approaching footsteps at least a thousand times. Once again, it was as if a protective angel kept him from being detected as he made his way back to the sleeping children. He woke them for their first bath since leaving England after removing his shirt, soaking it in the bucket and lathering it with soap. They were quick to remove their rags in the cool darkness of the rocking ship. He scrubbed their backs first, then behind their ears, rubbing hard on their lice-infected scalps; whereupon Dolly started to cry from the sting of lye in her eyes. Both Ever and her brother quieted her with soothing words to be still as Ever did his best to rinse the soap from her face. Ever had Buck finish bathing his sister before Buck cleaned himself in the hot water while Ever stood watch with his back to them for privacy. This would improve their chances of staying clear of disease, even though typhus would appear later with some.

Yesterday, Ever heard from the ship's cook that one of the crew had typhus and was quarantined by the captain to remain below deck where the gun powder was stored until they reached Virginia. Seaman Golly was ordered to deliver the man's food and water and after removing his waste bucket the deck seaman was to wash his hands in scalding water topside.

Now, once again the hardest part of the day was upon him, when he would sneak the children back to the hole at the bottom of the rope ladder in the sorriest of places where the moaning and groaning of the dying never ceased. This is when Ever would light a candle and check on every passenger to see if any had died during the night. Usually there was at least one and some days two, however today the light revealed that all were breathing. So, up he'd go, leaving Buck and Dolly in the

11

darkness that reeked of foul odors and the obstreperous snoring of the huddled poor Irish souls doing their best to hang on for another day.

Later he would return with food and water with the rising light of day that blinded all in the hole who cast their eyes upward. This was a sign they had survived another night with sweet Virginia getting closer yet seen by faith alone.

Ship of Death

Before sunset and just 3 days from Virginia, when Ever had finished his detail and climbed out of the Irish holding area, he saw and heard this calamity on deck with the crew scurrying about in this state of urgency he hadn't seen since leaving Liverpool. Off the starboard bow a few hundred yards away he saw a small clipper ship foundering without mast and bobbing on the sea with no visible crew on its deck.

Ever could see his captain using a spyglass, looking at the vessel that appeared to be abandoned with its masts down for some strange reason. The captain ordered a dinghy with oars be lowered and a crew of 8 armed with musket, pistol, and saber to investigate this mystery vessel. Ever was stunned when the captain ordered him to come along on this search and seizure mission. He would be used as a scout, to be the first to board, since he was the most expendable of The Dutchman's crew. Right before descending the rope ladder into the dinghy he was given a 6" hunting knife in a leather sheaf and handed a boatswain's hook that he would use to board the dead ship in the calm Atlantic once they were alongside.

Six men began rowing once the captain was aboard the dinghy. Ever was nervous about using this iron grappling hook for the first time with a large knife riding his hip. The sea was eerily calm; however, the smell of gun powder mixed with the

13

body smells of the crew made Ever more nervous with each thrusting oar of the men, who to a man did not envy the poor Irishman about to board the listless ship that to experience sailors had the distinct smell of dead flesh. As the rotting smell of death increased –so did the number of sharks circling the quiet ship, their glistening blue-black fins searching for fresh meat.

Although half the size of The Dutchman, Ever was aware that he had to heave the hook high and away so that it landed on the deck of the ship instead of dropping back down into the dinghy and possibly injuring the crew and himself. Aware that he was the lowest ranking man here, he was also aware that any one of these grizzled and armed men would sooner run him through than suffer from any injury caused by him. His throw had to be perfectly timed with both rocking vessels along with the uncertain wind blocked by the ship's hull.

"You better be right, lad, or this is as far as you go!" one grisly oarsman barked, while all the while their captain was aware that he alone had to lead this search for bounty among this bunch of thieves who would slit a man's throat for any bounty deemed worthy.

Everson stood up and started swinging the heavy hook over his head before heaving it high and forward with enough force to make sure the hook landed on the ship, whereupon he pulled the hook toward him until the hook was secured on something and adroitly climbed the rope with an alacrity that impressed the entire crew.

Once on deck he could see and smell the carnage of a few dead slaves as well as a few pirates he assumed were from the islands of The Americas. He called down to the captain that there appeared to be only casualties, no survivors. All the ship's masts were blown down from cannon shot. Ever secured the boarding rope ladder for the crew to climb, leaving one man on the dinghy for their departure. Golly hoped he would be ordered to the dinghy, for the carnage was cruel and the smell worse than the hell hole.

The grubby crew went about their business of scrounging for anything worth nabbing, including searching the dead for valuables, which didn't preclude them from looking for and cutting out gold teeth from one of the ship's dead crew. The Dutchman's captain discerned that this was a slave ship from Africa and headed for The Americas, but intercepted by island pirates known to steal slaves and then sell them to slave traders on the islands.

Nothing of value was on the ghost ship stripped clean by human vultures until only the bare bones were left on its hull. Then, one of the Dutchman's crew came up from below deck with a young African boy, an obvious child of slaves who'd been found in a galley storage compartment. Ever could see that the boy was about Buck's age and terrified. The boy wore only a piece of red cloth around his waist and was as thin as any boy Ever had ever seen, although the boy did not appear weak or of ill health. When it appeared to Ever as if the boy would be left alone on the ghost ship for fear of disease, Ever inspected the boy and addressed his captain: "He's not infected with typhus. The boy will die if we leave him here. Captain, I could use some help below deck to keep the ship clean. With but a few days remaining on our voyage I have more than enough rations to spare."

The captain paused, the whole crew watching and waiting for his response, whether to show mercy or not to this "slave boy" who would not look into the eyes of any of these white men he'd been taught to fear.

15

"Take the boy then! Keep him out of my sight and off my ship at first landing!" the captain barked at his deck seaman.

The captain's next order shocked Ever: "If the boy can swim he can stay in my holding area! I won't have his likes on my dinghy!

Ever looked out at The Dutchman looming so far away and had to say to the captain, "The sharks, Captain, he'll never make it that far!"

"Then he stays here," the captain's words cruel and final as he and his crew had a good laugh while disembarking back down to the dinghy.

Everson Golly stood beside the boy with not once thinking of leaving him here on this ship of death. He reached down and gently raised the boy's chin to communicate with the boy's eyes.

"Can you swim?" Ever then demonstrated by pointing to The Dutchman and made swimming strokes with his arms.

The boy knew right away what the white man was saying and nodded no, which made Ever swallow hard as the last man was off-boarding to board the dinghy. When the Irish deck seaman was to lower the iron hook to the dinghy and board himself, the crew watched in amazement when Ever called out to the captain, "We'll be swimming together, sir! Leave us a rope to climb when we get there!"

The captain could see the fins of sharks circling his dinghy.

"I'll not have my deck seaman become shark food over a boy sired by slaves! Come aboard Seaman Golly! That's an order!"

Ever turned back to the boy, who could've run away, but he didn't. Instead, the boy stood still trembling with fear from thoughts of going into the sea and not knowing how to swim.

"I have a plan, sir! We'll be there! Don't sail without us!"

Then: Golly left the crew's sight and the captain ordered his crew to row for The Dutchman.

The boy watched the white man with red hair go over to one of the dead pirates and drag the dead body to the other side of the ship, then with all his strength he lifted then dropped the corpse into the ocean in order to distract the sharks to give them a chance in the water. Not wanting to watch frenzied sharks tear into the dead flesh, he looked for another body, finding an old black slave that had been killed and not taken because of his age. The boy knew this African man from his village; he had been nice to the boy's mother and remembered the old man giving his mother bread on the ship more than once. And now: he watched the white man push the old man into the sea. Exhausted, Ever found the nearest dead man, a member of the crew. This man was much bigger than the first two and when the boy saw Ever struggling to move the dead body –the boy came over and helped lift and push the body into the sea.

Both of them looked down at the shark feast, what seemed like a hundred sharks thrashing about in a smorgasbord feeding frenzy. Breathing hard and not wanting to waste time, for fear the captain would sail without them, Ever removed his knife from its sheath and cut long swaths from the ship's mast and tied them together to make a long piece of fabric he secured so they could climb down quietly into the water on the other side of the ship that appeared clear of sharks. No way could they jump in and attract attention. He motioned for the boy to come over to him, whereupon the boy thought about running away until he

17

saw the exhausted man with the red hair drop to his knees and put his hands together as if in prayer, something his mother taught him to do. Now the man motioned for the boy to come to him upon seeing the dinghy closing in on the mother ship. The boy walked over to him. Ever prepared to descend to the water and motioned for the boy to climb onto his back and hold onto him as Ever put the handle of his knife between his teeth. The boy rode piggyback as they moved closer and then into the water ever so quietly while the sharks feeding on the other side of the ship intensified.

Once in the cool salty sea Ever pushed them away from the ship with his feet, a glide as silent as possible without kicking, then a wide butterfly stroke, the swimmer's head going under water then up for air in a gasping inhalation all the while his teeth biting down hard on the weapon he hoped he didn't have to use. The boy held his breathe, taking breaths when he could with his head resting on the man's back and holding his hands around his neck for dear life.

There were no fins ahead of him, so Ever found it easier to keep his eyes closed and unaware of how far he had to go. After fifty yards or so he started to kick more and more to help his speed and take some of the load from his arms. This was amazing human will to survive, to keep plowing through the water, to not think of fatigue. All because he knew he was swimming for more than two lives. The image of Buck and Dolly huddled together were there, below deck on that ship he just had to reach. Yet after a while his body and the boy's weight were draining him with so far to go. He was swallowing sea water now and then, forcing him to grab his knife from his teeth quick before he coughed and lost his only weapon forever. He grabbed and fisted the handle in his dominant left hand with the blade pointing away from him as he continued stroking and now breathing freely as he could feel his passenger's entire body trembling all over his aching back.

Meanwhile the captain was back on board his ship and watching his brave deck seaman with his spyglass. He could see the boy on his back with yet so far to go. Then: the captain moved his magnified lens behind his deck seaman and could see the ominous blue-black, blade-shaped fin of a shark moving closer to the poor lads. He looked down to his oarsmen waiting in the dinghy for his orders, whether to go back for them.

Ever saw the shark's fin off to his left and kept swimming with renewed strength from adrenaline caused by his worst fear. With every swimming stroke he was ready to stab the shark if it came within his reach. The menacing killer began circling them, and when Ever felt it's slick-wet razor skin brush by his foot –he had to stop and face it while the boy held on.

"Hold on tight!" Ever yelled while treading water and following the ever-closing shark. His left arm was ready; he waited for the right moment and timed his stab deep into the shark's cold-black eye, causing the 6-foot-long killer to thrash about and disappear down into the ocean. Instead of waiting, Ever continued swimming for that beautiful ship he had cursed a thousand times for its cruelty. Sadly, it didn't seem to him that he was even half-way to The Dutchman.

"God, if you get us to that ship in one piece, I'll be the best man I can be!" Ever swore out loud between gasping breaths. "I know I've said that a thousand times before, but this time I mean it, God! Please, don't take us this way!

On he swam until he felt a thump on his lower right leg and then a sharp pain; a different shark was chewing on his calf muscle, which caused the terrified boy to wrap his legs around

19

Ever's waist. Ever stabbed downward and into the shark's snout and kept digging his blade in so the devil fish would release its bite, which it did.

Now, he knew his blood would bring the sharks in greater numbers as he looked behind them and saw three fins headed straight for them from the slave ship. He had to stop swimming and face them. They circled him, his blood inviting them closer and closer. Just when he was about to stab the nearest shark: the glorious sound of a musket went off, a lead ball blasting clear through the nearest shark, splashing dead shark all over Ever and the slave boy. The sound of a well-aimed harpoon impaled another shark. Ever turned to see one of the men in the dinghy chop off the impaled shark's head with a machete and hook the shark meat into the boat with the aid of the man with the musket.

Two of the oarsmen helped Ever and the boy onto the dinghy. Ever's calf was bleeding bad from the awful shark bite that covered at least six inches on his right calf. One of the oarsman removed his scarf from his neck and wrapped it around the wound to abate the bleeding. The boy was trembling and in shock from the near-death experience, looking at this brave white man who was injured and exhausted.

The slave boy knew he had to be in better hands now, compared to the pirates who had taken his mother. It was nearly a year ago when his mother had given him the English name, "James," knowing the day was coming when they would be shipped to America to work in the cotton and tobacco fields. James had no last name, yet the night before he and his mother along with forty others of their race were herded onto the slave ship in Africa, the same ship he could now see getting smaller and smaller, he had given himself his last name: "Virginia," named after their original destination.

20

Upon reaching The Dutchman, from his quarterdeck the Captain watched his deck seaman helped aboard from the dinghy, his wound attended to by the ship's cook. The slave boy was escorted to the Irish holding area where now some 140 passengers languished. Ever kept his eye on the boy until he was out of sight and thanked God several times for their safe return.

Sweet Virginia

The last thing Everson Golly remembered before passing out was the incredibly biting sting of pain on his leg when the ship's cook poured whiskey on his wound before dressing it with a clean bandage. The pain was so excruciating he bit through the wooden soup ladle clenched between his teeth, whereupon he slept for twelve straight hours.

Before sunrise, Ever awoke on the dark hull-creaking deck of The Dutchman, a ceaseless rocking place he once detested, and a place he'd never prayed so hard for to set foot on again. Until his ordeal in the shark-infested ocean –he had never feared death to that degree. Perhaps that's why he slept so long and hard: every muscle in his body had been worked to its maximum capacity; he believed his very bones would've popped out of his skin if he had survived the sharks and had to swim all the way to The Dutchman.

Thoughts of the slave boy below deck made him turn onto his left side to inspect his bandaged wound that covered nearly half of the back of his right calf. He got to his knees and managed to pull himself up to his feet by grabbing the same dinghy that plucked him and the boy from the jaws of death. He owed his life to those men, including the Captain who had to have ordered them back to get them.

Aware of his promise to God, he unlocked the latch to the hell hole; he was curious if the passengers had been fed and watered in his absence. Right away he could smell that it had not been swabbed since he last made his rounds. Slowly he had to painfully make his way down the rope ladder by putting his weight only on his left leg and using his arms to help. Before reaching the dark deck of the hole he could see the wide-eyed gaze of Buck and Dolly close to the ladder and hear the God-awful snoring coming from the half-dead passengers.

"Fetch me a candle Buck and light it for me."

Buck went over to the hiding place where they stowed the candles and flint.

"How are you, Dolly?" Ever whispered to the little girl, who looked happy to see him although she did not appear to him to be feeling well.

Buck came over to Ever and his sister with the lit candle, holding its brass candleholder in front of him.

"Did they feed and water you last night?" he asked the lad.

Buck nodded no. The smell of the unvented place told Ever that none of the waste buckets had been emptied. Buck lowered the candle to see the bandage on Ever's leg.

"I got bit by a hungry shark and I'm fit as a fiddle," Ever whispered, feeling thrilled to be alive. He took the candle from the lad and inspected Buck and Dolly's arms, thankful not a red spot to be seen, and saying, "Bucklin Dunn, I've got a job for you, lad." Then: Ever remembered the slave boy and asked Buck if he'd seen the boy. Buck pointed to a dark space behind them on the other side of the ladder. Before Ever and Buck went to find the boy, Ever bent down to Dolly's little face and noticed her dimpled chin for the first time in the candlelight. He smiled into her sky-blue eyes and whispered, "Wait here. I have a new

23

friend for you." He wasn't sure she understood him, yet her little mouth had this calmness all around it that emanated from her trusting eyes, also calm and glad to see him.

Ever then Buck saw the wide, unblinking eyes of the slave boy; he was sitting on his haunches with his bare back against the bulkhead. The rescued boy could never be afraid of the man who saved his life. He could only smile back at Ever in the flickering yellow-gold candlelight when his eyes saw the blood-stained bandage on his leg. Like Ever: the slave boy self-named "James Virginia" was also thrilled to be alive. That near-death experience made them both more alive than ever.

Ever explained to Buck that this special boy would be his helper, and to show him how we bring the waste buckets up the ladder, "since my leg pains me dearly."

"I'll be topside. The buckets will be heavier now. I want you both to carry one at a time up the ladder to me."

Buck nodded that he understood.

"Good. Now I expect you lads to work hard and I will bring each of you an extra ration of bread and water for your good labor. We'll do the same in the morning with bread and water until my leg's better. Now get the boy and take the candle with you until you get to the ladder with each bucket. I'll be able to swab the deck, and will use your help to hold the candle and move the water bucket. Do you understand me, Bucklin Dunn?"

"Yes," the boy said with an earnest determination that made Ever laugh, perhaps the first sound of laughter this place had heard since leaving England.

Buck walked over to the slave boy and motioned for him to come with him. Ever watched the boys walk over to the area

24

where the waste buckets were stowed in steerage, then gingerly made the climb favoring his left leg while using his arm strength, all the while knowing that by putting the slave boy to work, it would diminish protests from the passengers not wanting to berth in the same space with an African slave boy who could carry a new disease from his country. By helping to keep their space clean, Ever reasoned that fears would be overlooked for improved sanitation; and, with only two days of sailing remaining on their voyage –the African orphan would be on his own with a new start.

For the next 2 days and anxious nights passengers and crew were moving about and preparing their legs for "sweet Virginia," the name given to the American state and representing to all the end of a long voyage. Yet something insidious was going on in the hell hole. An elderly man had died from typhus in the hell hole the day Ever was injured and his body discovered by the boys when serving the daily bread and water. Because of his injury Ever petitioned the Captain for help hoisting the dead man out of the holding area. The Captain declined, not willing to risk typhus contact with his men. *"You'll have to get help from passengers,"* the Captain waved him away, suffering from a hangover and not wanting the deck seaman around him now.

Not one male passenger volunteered assistance in removing the dead body after Ever's supplication to them from topside. Now he had to make his way down the rope ladder with a throbbing leg that was not allowing him good rest and seemed to be getting worse with time. *Thank God for the lads,* Ever thought, never failing to praise them or bring extra bread and water for the good work they were doing together since his injury. Upon reaching the area where the men languished with illness, he could see the men shrinking away, trying to be invisible and avoid the gruesome detail of removing the dead

25

man out of here. Yet Ever spoke to the men from his heart: "I can see sweet Virginia. If we don't get the dead body out of here and into the sea they'll quarantine the ship and won't let you off-board for days or even weeks I'm told. I need one man to go topside to pull the hoist and two men to load him into the hoist. I suggest we get to this before we all call this our permanent home."

Three men volunteered without delay, all haggard and emaciated from malnutrition and lack of fresh air and sunlight. They moved like old and infirm men, about to collapse from lack of energy. Every shuffling step they took in their ragged clothes made one believe they were beggars on their last leg. Because of their laying around like lazy dogs the entire voyage, their movement was precarious to say the least and seemed like cruel punishment given to beaten men. Even Buck and the African boy helped these tired men load the body onto a 4'x1' slab of timber that Ever and a volunteer hoisted down by a pulley with two attached ropes held in place by grooves under the wooden plank that had managed to lift some three dozen dead passengers since leaving England 42 days ago.

Everson hoped this was the last passenger to be shark food as he and his helper rolled the corpse over the side and heard that ominous splash. Both men paused to stand looking at the mouth of the 20-mile-wide Chesapeake Bay. "Sweet Virginia," the helper grinned at Ever's agreeing smile. They watched for any signs of life on the distant pier head in this busy harbor, able to see other ships docked as well as every kind of vessel coming and going by the score. Ever looked behind him and the whole crew seemed to be watching and pointing out landmarks as The Dutchman approached "sweet Virginia" in the calmest and bluest of seas since leaving Liverpool. Wincing from the recent stress he'd put on his leg, he knew he had to see a doctor right away upon off-boarding, for green and yellow pus had replaced blood on his dirty bandage that hadn't been changed since the injury. And he had seen red spots on his belly and chest upon examining himself in the Captain's shaving mirror this morning.

He wished he could bring the three children topside now to see this splendid view that they had to be longing for as much as anyone on the ship. His body was becoming weaker from his mind telling him to walk off this ship as soon as it docked, not exposing himself to anyone, especially the children —if indeed he did have the dreaded early symptoms of typhus. He thought Dolly's eyes looked as if she was ill since the wide sky blueness had been weakened a degree of blue by the slowing of her blinking eyelids and the warmth of her forehead had risen to the early stage of a fever. Thoughts of Dolly needing medical attention made him most anxious to remove her from the ship and find a doctor to treat her. He had his money his father made him sew into his trousers; he could use that money for the doctor and getting the four of them some good food for their frail bodies. He reasoned: *"What good is the money if it's found by the undertaker?"*

Yes, Everson Golly was thinking for the four of them now. He had promised God to care for all three of them if he ever made it to Virginia. And there it was: "Sweet Virginia," he whispered. His father had heard from American merchant men visiting a Dublin pub that land was free in the western part of Virginia close to the West Virginia border where the Appalachian and Allegheny Mountains ran together, some 60 miles north of a town named Big Lick. He would go there with his new ready-made family to stake his claim and make a home for them. This journey had strengthened his faith in God, as often happens when there's so much danger all around. Surely, he believed, to spare us was a calling that we were meant to be together on this new land.

The crew was making ready the ship to enter the busy mouth of the Chesapeake Bay and to the pier head of the James River before docking in Norfolk. Everson knew the exact instant he would gather the children and off-board with them before the Captain could stop them. No way was he staying one second longer on this ship when Dolly needed medical attention as soon as possible.

Journey of Heart

Everson was to carry Dolly to the nearest doctor sixteen miles away in Suffolk, Virginia. He had the boys begin their journey holding hands, following; but that didn't last long in this blinding light of day for the children, who had to shield their sensitive eyes from the blinding sun in busy Norfolk. It was in this sun-brightness that Ever could see that Dolly and Buck had the red spots of typhus on their arms and bellies. He could only assume the quiet African boy contacted the dreaded disease on The Dutchman. Far too many appeared sick and wretched in Norfolk to even consider looking for a doctor in that disease-infested place. So he inquired at a nearby livery stable where might be the nearest doctor outside Norfolk. A jolly good man told Ever about a doctor in Suffolk named Grady. *An Irishman,* Ever thought, *a good sign.* The doctor would be easy to find if he stayed on this road, where *"you can see Doctor Grady's office on the town square as clear as day,"* the livery man smiled while pointing the way.

Then, it had to happen sooner or later: not far from the livery a group of slaves were bound together by chains and being auctioned off to a group of white planters. It occurred to Ever that any of those slaves could come from the same place where the boy was from, and perhaps some were family. He watched the boy's reaction as they neared the slaves bound together. Instead of trying to ask the boy if he knew any of them, Ever purposely led them over to the human auction, to parade the boy

29

in front of them to see their reaction. None of them appeared to recognize the boy, since Ever noticed that every single man and woman looked at him.

Near the human auction was where Ever stopped to look at his injured leg, removing his bandage to expose a terrible wound that was infected and in danger of gangrene. He left his pant leg rolled up and above his wound to give it fresh air and he dabbed it with water. Then, he grabbed the African boy by his shoulders, pointed his finger at the boy's heart and then pointed to the slaves as if asking if he knew any of them. The boy nodded no with a big smile. They had to see that doctor in Suffolk, so they continued walking.

***

Suffolk had been a dead end. Doctor Grady had been summoned to Richmond to treat victims of a terrible fire at a garment factory, and wasn't expected back at his office for some time. It was in Suffolk where Ever was informed he could catch a ride west to Big Lick in Petersburg 60 miles northwest of Suffolk on a wagon train. Every third day the empty wagons took on passengers for a modest fee. And there was bound to be a doctor in Petersburg or Richmond, the state's capital and largest city. The same generous woman in Doctor Grady's office who gave Ever directions and the information about the salt wagons to Big Lick also gave the four new Virginians a bag of green apples and a larger goatskin water container filled with fresh water for their 2-day walk to Petersburg "*if you walk ten to twelve hours a day,*" the woman told the young Irishman with the bad limp and three sorry-looking children.

A few miles outside of Suffolk the foursome stopped for the night and slept under an old chestnut tree that was far enough from the main road so other travelers wouldn't see them. To this

30

point they'd seen hundreds of vagabonds and desperate-looking men on this road to Petersburg. It was also here, their first real respite since leaving the ship that they had their first taste of Virginia green apples. None of the Irish felt like much more than one bite; yet the African boy seemed to enjoy his apple and even another. They all drank good water from the goatskin container, and for the first time since Liverpool Ever really felt like he was in his new home country, the place he would spend the rest of his life.

Now they must sleep to recover their legs. Ever realized these kids needed him to survive. He was afraid to look at his throbbing wound under his pant leg knowing there was nothing he could do now…but sleep. Sleeping on solid earth was so good for them compared to the ever-changing undulations of the sea. Now, Ever could breathe in the cool spring air of May in Virginia and tell his mind that they would all improve with time now that they were away from the wretchedly sick on The Dutchman. Silent prayers came from his lips, asking God to allow the children to awaken without fever, as the warm skin from Dolly's arm against his seemed to be warmer than yesterday. Never in his life had he prayed so much for others since leaving Ireland. His father told him he would, reminding him often that *"hardships to come will test your faith."*

In the cool shade of sundown when he could hear the light breath of sleep coming from three small faces, faces he was growing fonder of by the day –he felt it safe to cry, to release some of the emotional storms of anguish and fear he had experienced on the arduous passage to Virginia. Salty tears moistened his dry lips when he gave thanks to God for their safe arrival. He prayed for the strength and courage to care for the children; and he prayed that none of these children die from the typhus fever that he'd seen cause so much death on The Dutchman.

***

An hour before sunrise all four were up and moving their legs toward Petersburg. At Blackwater Creek they replenished their water supply and Ever soaked his bandaged leg in the cold water. He could see under the pus-colored cloth that his leg was not healing; it was festering with the green, black and yellow colors of danger that needed medical attention. There was no doctor in these parts of Virginia obscurities, only this hard mud-caked road that led to what they needed in Petersburg. Several times with tiny Dolly in his arms and the boys following his steady pace behind him, he'd often call out to them, asking if they were hungry yet. The answer was "*no*" from Buck, his face and fine red hair wet with perspiration from fever. The slave boy, even thinner than Buck, seemed unaffected by the walk: he'd take but a sip of water whenever they stopped to rest, compared to the thirsty gulps of his Irish companions. Dolly also would nod no if Ever inquired if she was hungry. Each time she did so was a heart-wrenching thing for Ever to see, this sadness of a baby girl who wanted nothing now but to feel better.

Ever had washed the green and white scarf he had removed from their mother's dead body at the creek where they last got water. He had it wrapped with his bundle of meagre possessions he carried in a tote sack over his shoulder, not wanting to give it to the girl until he'd washed it in the creek. He managed to put the cool scarf around the top of her little head without her seeing that it was her mother's scarf.

It was obvious to Everson Golly that he was using the children to give him strength; frequent praying to be a strong man, one who could lead them to a place where they could

32

regain their health. Ten miles south of Petersburg and every step on Virginia soil reminded him that he was indeed in a new country just over seventy years old. Black slaves, drifter field hands, and white indentured servants of all ages were planting tobacco and cotton in fields as vast as all of Dublin. Now, Ever wasn't strong enough for any kind of work; all he could manage was a plodding walk…one foot…then another for a mile or so, then they'd all rest after a sip of water.

Any wagons were jammed with people and supplies coming or going from the markets in Richmond. Another night of quick sleep beside the road; at dawn they continued on at a slower pace yet were all aware they could reach Petersburg today and be on a wagon headed for the salt mines of Big Lick in western Virginia.

Outside Petersburg they were given directions to the salt wagons from a traveler they'd met when they stopped to rest their sore feet and clean up a bit in this icy-cold creek that ran along a field that had been recently planted by the looks of the footprints of workers in the muddy soil between the endless rows. It was here that Ever raised his pant leg and removed the filthy cloth, now exposing the torn and missing flesh the shark had taken. He soaked his injured leg in the cold water up to his knee. It was here that Buck could see just how bad his injury was. Buck whispered something to his sister, which caused her to give up her mother's scarf. Buck handed the scarf to Ever. Ever thanked them for the new bandage and secured it around his wound. This was when Ever asked the slave boy his name by pointing to himself and saying "Ever"; then he pointed to Dolly and Buck and said their names. All three waited for the slave boy to say his name but nothing came, until Ever started to get to his feet.

"James…Virginia," the African boy said from memory, this English name his mother made him memorize.

"James Virginia," Ever smiled down at the boy, whose big-toothed carefree smile made the Irish trio laugh together for the first time since leaving Europe.

The remaining trek to Petersburg was now filled with Ever constantly calling out his name as well as "James Virginia" and the other kids' names so all the children knew everyone's name. And Ever would call out each name in song, a paternal tactic he used in order to get their minds off mounting fevers that Ever knew could last up to a week.

"Pretty little Dolly/ Carried by Everson Golly/ James in Virginia/ Named James Virginia/ There goes Bucklin/Walks like a ducklin'!"

Before long he had them all singing that silly little song while plodding over a land they could not call "home". And it didn't matter to their leader if anyone was around them on this road to Petersburg, for he would belt out his song even louder, which made the children, even James join in. This kind of behavior was atypical of the young man from Dublin who was thought of by locals there as "queer quiet"— and even his father thought the same.

Upon seeing the church spires of Petersburg poking above the hills, that's when Ever became clear about two valuable lessons he'd learned since leaving home: that suffering is a choice whether in silence or constant complaining; and, for the man who celebrates in gratitude all things that come his way – the spirit will always move the body away from pain.

***

Again, any doctor in Petersburg was summoned to the Richmond disaster; there was no doctor to be found on these verdant hills that ran along the southern border of the capital city. There was no time to be disappointed, for Ever heard from many among The Dutchman crew that there's no cure for typhus; "*it either kills you or it doesn't.*"

It was his leg that Ever wanted treated, for gangrene was more deadly than typhus; and, he was aware that if left untreated, at the very least he could lose his leg. Now, he feared being a one-legged cripple with three children to support. There was no time to dwell on finding a doctor, since he found out that the salt wagons were close and soon to be headed for Big Lick in western Virginia, a town that surely had to have a doctor that hadn't been called away to Richmond.

Off they walked, to cover the mile or so to reach the salt wagons. They were now in the heart of those horrific tales of slavery in the Americas that circulated about Dublin for as long as Ever could remember. There were the lashings and hangings, and dogs hunting down runaways as if they were animals to be kept in bondage. And yet, Ever remembered his father's warnings about indentured servants who were nothing more than white slaves contracted to work for wealthy American planters and businessmen. Many of these Irish men paid for their passage by signing a contract to work in the American cotton and tobacco fields, manufacturing plants, and even the salt wells around Big Lick. His father told him how terrible the working conditions were for those men, and he wanted his son to have nothing to do with this kind of "*white slavery.*"

On their walk to the salt wagons Ever could see the telling faces of the slaves and the white people, and how James Virginia could be a problem for their ride west. That's when Ever had the idea to give James one of his three coins, "to keep it safe in your fist until you use it to pay for our ride to Big Lick." Ever could see that James didn't understand why he'd been given a silver coin, more treasure than the boy had ever held in his hand.

35

James did understand that he was to hold onto the coin in his fisted hand because he did know the coin was a valuable thing.

A team of four mules was hitched to each of the five wagons destined for the salt mines of Big Lick. The wagon master was a big red-faced Irishman wearing a floppy black leather hat that didn't conceal a missing right ear that had been sliced off in a Dublin tavern fight when he was a young man. The man was smitten by little Dolly and could see they were all in need of a ride. Ever had James give the coin to the wagon boss, and without a word spoken in protest about a slave boy riding in one of his wagons, the man said to the foursome: "You ride in wagon five at the rear. We roll in one hour."

"Thank you, sir," Ever was grateful, "and might there be water nearby?"

"There's a rain barrel over there," the man pointed at the oak barrel then winked at the lass in Ever's arms.

Ever loaded the children in the last wagon then walked to the rain barrel to replenish their water supply. All three kids watched his every move. They saw him at the barrel splashing water on his face and neck and soon let out this guttural sigh from exhaustion. He knew he'd been losing his strength every day since the shark attack and wasn't sure how much longer his leg could go before it was too late. Upon filling the water container he raised his soiled pant leg to have a look. He removed the mother's scarf and saw that his wound was turning black at both ends of the bite. Instead of soaking the scarf in the barrel of rain water he palmed and splashed water from the barrel onto the scarf and wrung it out. Before securing the cool, damp scarf to his leg he palmed water onto his wound and hoped for the best, reminding his mind to be optimistic around the children. *"There's a doctor in Big Lick,"* was his mind-set now.

It wasn't long on the road before the four passengers in wagon five knew it was going to be one rough and rocky ride for many miles. The mule teams kept about the same pace as humans walking, so Ever figured it would take two long days of this torturous rumbling and shaking without sleep, since each wagon had a second driver resting in back and waiting for their turn to take the reins for twelve hours.

The spare drivers slept most of the way, and they smelled like dirty animals. *"Worse than a skunk!"* one driver commented, and insisted he ride in back with the slave boy. Ever hoped James could not understand the drivers' rough language, but Buck did understand the men.

About every three hours the wagon train would stop so that the drivers could have a bathroom break and roll a smoke. Ever made sure the kids had privacy when they did their "business" in the bucket hanging over the side at the back of the wagon. The kids slept more than Ever did; and in many ways this part of their journey was the hardest. No matter how bone-jarring uncomfortable it was riding on this mud-rutted road – *"at least my feet feel better,"* Ever would laugh and poke his finger through the soles of his shoes, which made the children giggle.

When the older first driver came to the wagon bed to sleep and the "skunk" began his 12-hour shift at the reins, the haggard driver gruffly ordered confused James to the rear of the wagon, *"as far as possible away from me."* Everson, growing hotter and weaker with fever, stepped in and moved James to the back of the wagon, not wanting anything to jeopardize their ride to Big Lick. When Ever had taken James's hand, he noticed that the boy's skin was warmer and felt his forehead for a fever. Now it was obvious that James had the same fever they all had. He gave the lean boy with the slower blinking brown eyes a drink of water and he had James lie down with his head resting on Ever's thigh.

By nightfall it was obvious that sleep would be all but impossible on this bouncing rattletrap ride to western Virginia. Half-way there: it started to rain hard until they were eventually covered by a cowhide tarp that was stowed with other supplies in the lead wagon. This was when the driver's took their dinner break. The sick family of four in wagon #5 stayed in the wagon with no appetites from the fever Ever kept concealed from the drivers for fear of being booted off.

The further west they went the more rocking and rolling the roads became. Near the end of day two was when Ever's injured leg seemed to be throbbing the most, just when the vast Blue Ridge Mountains could be seen as dark and imposing obstacles on the distant horizon. Along the Blue Ridge and south to North Carolina was where the squatter land began; beyond them was the salt town of Big Lick. Beyond that: the Appalachian and Allegheny Mountains. Here, at the beginning of South Gap is where Ever decided to go off alone when the mule team stopped to rest; he would limp north into the woods of the Blue Ridge and die alone on land he'd dreamed of before losing his leg to a doctor's knife in Big Lick. He'd seen his share of one-legged men in Dublin, *and they were all beggars. No life for me,* he'd decided. Before he died he wanted to see the land he envisioned for so long. When he managed to get himself out of the wagon he took his remaining two coins and gave one to Buck and the other to James, explaining to them: "I have to find my land alone. There's no other way. Use the money to find a doctor in Big Lick and the doctor will help you find a place that's safe." Then, Ever gave the water container to Buck, telling him to find fresh drinking water in Big Lick.

"I want to go with you, Everson Golly," Buck protested by trying to get out of the wagon, but Ever stopped him, firmly telling him, "No, Buck. You must stay with your sister where people can help you. And James will stay with you because he's your brother now. Do you understand me, lad?" Ever's voice faltered, his physical and emotional pain he did not want the children to see as he was certain he was a walking dead man.

The children watched him limp away from the wagon, soon leaving the road that led to Big Lick and vanishing in the dense forest. It was James who made the first move by getting out of the wagon while clutching the coin in his fisted hand. On the ground he looked up at the wide-eyed Buck and Dolly; he tried to hand his coin to Buck and was frustrated because he wanted to tell them how he had to go with the man who saved his life. Instead of taking the coin, Buck picked up his sister and handed her down to James before exiting the wagon. Each boy took Dolly by the hand and they headed for the spot where Ever had disappeared into the woods.

Not far into the tree-line they saw poor Ever sitting with his back against a tree; he was shivering from fever and sobbing from leaving the children behind. Upon seeing their spooked faces walking over to him, Ever struggled to his knees, continuing to sob while embracing them all at once as rain began to patter on the leaves above them. The boys gave him back his coins and he laughed upon returning both coins to Buck, saying, "Let's go find us a home."

A Splash in Darkness

James found a piece of a fallen branch that he gave to Ever to use as a walking stick, a remarkable aid and much appreciated by a man who was literally on his last leg and fading. The boys took turns carrying Dolly through the thick vegetation. It was getting more and more difficult to stay in any one direction for long. By the time they rested their sore feet in a small creek and replenished their water supply, the sun was setting on the other side of the mountain, bringing a cool darkness that increased Ever's fever to a shivering nightmare he did not want the children to see.

Ever wanted to climb higher on this eastern side of the mountain, however he was unable to ascend unless at a gradual angle where the forest permitted. He told the children in a delirious state of fever that he wanted his land to be near the summit of a mountain and facing east, *"so I can see the sun coming up over Ireland,"* he must've stated a hundred times before they stopped to sleep for the night.

Buck gave Ever sips of water and poured palm-sized pools of water onto the dying man's hot face and neck. Combined with his increasing fever and spreading gangrene that had moved to his foot and thigh of his injured leg, all the kids laid upon his chest in the cold darkness of a spring night praying his shivering would stop.

Buck cried later that night when Dolly was asleep, for the boy had seen these final stages of the dying in the bowels of The Dutchman. Buck feared losing this man as he had feared losing his mother, and once again they'd be all alone in a new world they knew nothing about.

On The Dutchman, Ever had heard from the salty crew that in Virginia slaves were sold and moved deeper south into the Carolinas and Georgia. Because of James, Ever had turned north upon leaving the wagon, wanting the boy to follow his lead some day in order to stay clear of the whippings and hangings he'd read about in Dublin newspapers so frequently.

Now: Ever opened his eyes as if to see this world for one last time. The moon was full directly above the tree where they lie, and yet he couldn't see it for the trees. He could feel the warm sleeping heads of the children tucked tight against his shivering body. Everson Golly was barely a young man and felt as helpless as these children had to feel with him as their leader. Dying right here where they would find him seemed so cruel to him that he summoned all his strength to get up and away without waking the children. With his walking stick he made his way in the moonlight, threading his way through the dense forest for what seemed like miles, and yet was nothing close to that distance. He was so exhausted and burning up with fever that he could no longer hold onto the walking stick with even both hands, so he let it drop to the earth and couldn't resist falling with it onto his knees. Then: between his heavy breaths he heard the sweet sound of water rushing over rocks. He held his breath to gauge where it was coming from. It was over and beyond that hill to the west. He used the stick to get to his feet and made his way in the darkness up the hill…falling…then crawling on arms and legs, giving all he had left to reach the top of that hill to find the place where he could die alone and not be discovered.

41

Closer and closer to the sound of the water, and now he kept seeing the bodies of the dead he had hauled up from hell and pushed overboard into the sea. Then: he could see the plaintive face of Buck and Dolly's mother looking into his eyes before she died, as if pleading to watch over her children. Now, in his blind crawl toward the sound of water he saw the mother's lifeless body he hoisted topside to be delivered to the sea, all the while praying that her children did not hear the splash her body made into the dark ocean.

He had always heard that your life passed before you so fast just before you die –and it was. Clawing and climbing as if not wanting to leave this world without a fight, he kept on until now he was delirious and imagined he was once again a boy with the emerald hills of Ireland all around him. The dark hills were folding all around him as a boy when he walked to Shaney Pond at night in summertime to cool his body. Now, he removed his shirt as he clawed his way up to the last hill where on the other side a cold oasis awaited while the relentless vegetation of the Blue Ridge cut and scraped and scratched his upper body that was now covered by the red spots of typhus fever. By now his injured leg felt like a petrified slab of dead meat that could only be dragged over the earth until it hopefully just fell off his body. In the wagon he noticed the stench of gangrene. If the drivers hadn't smelled like dirty animals he might've noticed the foul odor of his rotting flesh. And yet: *"What could I have done?"*

He continued clawing his way uphill on all fours, avoiding the oak-hickory trees and not wanting to stop until he reached the top of this unforgiving hill, and then: he'd let gravity roll him down and into the water that he knew was on the other side. No more pain, for approaching death was the anodyne for Everson Golly, this merciful gift given to men who were about to leave this world of pain and suffering. On he climbed, all but dead

42

already; now seeing his body from high above, he could see the land appeared to flatten to an open space lit by silver moonlight. He hopped on one leg then dragged the other leg toward this void of darkness ahead, not knowing where this other side of the hill would lead him or how far it dropped into darkness. Then: he made his final physical act before dying and let his body fall into the unknown. Rolling, rolling, and tumbling in darkness over stone and shrub and flesh-tearing earth, all the while relaxing his body and letting his weight fall down the hill, his last moments on this painful earth...until...a splash in darkness.

Alone at Dawn...then Mulberries

The next morning James woke up bleary-eyed, his fever still with him as it was with the other children; and, the coin Ever gave him was still in his clenched hand. He looked around for Everson and even his walking stick was gone. James moved Buck's shoulder, waking him. Buck too was concerned that Ever was nowhere to be seen. Both boys looked for clues, some kind of trail their injured leader left in the night. Dolly's head was resting on the goatskin water vessel when her brother woke her. She was confused that Ever was gone. James secured the water container around his waist as Ever had done, then James gave Buck the coin Ever had given him, since Buck could put it inside his trouser pockets with the other coin.

Although their fevers appeared to be coming down, their hunger increased. They had no food and they were alone at dawn. James tried to find tracks and signs of Ever's direction while Dolly rode her brother's hip following the African boy's stalking, sweeping movements as if an experienced African hunter. They moved along the oak-hickory forest where hemlock and mixed-oak all but gave the impression that this was more than just another pine forest; this was the Blue Ridge at its best, where a billion trees played with color and light over four seasons.

Just when James thought he'd lost the trail uphill –he saw Ever's walking stick and like a true hunter he knew where to go after picking up the cane. Then: James listened to the sound of water just below the bird noise above him. It was sound that boiling water makes, and it was coming from the other side of this hill. He then found and picked up Ever's discarded, rumpled rag of a shirt.

Buck followed James up the hill and became hopeful upon seeing those big white teeth smiling while waving Ever's shirt and stick at them, letting them know that they were on the right trail. Upon seeing that Buck was struggling carrying his sister up the hill, James came back down and took Dolly in his arms so Buck could stop to rest and then continue to the hilltop. James put Dolly down once at the top of the hill so they could all rest and get a drink of water. They couldn't see any water down on the other side of the hill through the trees, and could not hear the same sound of bubbling water because of Dolly's crying from hunger.

Upon securing the water vessel and Ever's shirt around his waist, James started down the hill. He angled his descent and moved sideways down the slope of the hill while scanning the base of every tree for his friend as the sound of burbling water increased. Over rough ground on calloused feet that had never worn shoes –James had to find the man who saved his life. Then: a clearing revealed a valley of perhaps 2 square miles of prime land. James had to slide and scoot down on his rump because of the steep decline. It was too late to change his angle of descent and he started to tumble then fall into a pool of warm water that was deep enough to take the force of his weight. The pool was a fathom deep in places and James managed to land in the deeper part of the pool where he had to thrash about until he could touch bottom with his head out of the water. Since he couldn't swim he stayed near the edge of the pool; that's when he spotted Ever on the other side of this oasis of warm water that was bubbling and steaming at the surface. Ever was near this source of hot springs face-down, most of his body in the water with his head resting on a rock and arms spread-eagle as if he'd died that way from falling from the slope. James couldn't see through the steam to know whether Ever was alive or not, his face was turned away. He couldn't swim over to him, so he moved along the bank submerged like a crocodile until he could get to Ever.

"Is he alive?" Buck shouted, forgetting James spoke no English. Buck had put Dolly down on the slope to rest with her after taking a better angle than James had.

"Everson Golly," James shook Ever by his shoulder.

Ever lifted his cheek from the rock and turned to James, smiling and waving for the boy to get into the water with him. Ever put his arm around James, holding him close and wanting the boy to soak in the healing waters that had killed his fever and brought feeling back to his injured leg. Then Ever waved Buck and Dolly into the pool, telling them to "Come in!" First Buck jumped into the warm water and then took Dolly into his arms, bathing together, their first real bath since leaving Europe. Soon, the soothing water was bringing laughter to Buck and his sister, and now James was feeling the salubrious effect of the healing springs on his tingling skin. Ever told them again to submerge their heads completely, and for Buck to scrub Dolly's scalp with the healing water to kill the head lice once and for all.

Now Ever had reason to celebrate as James gave Ever his walking stick when Ever addressed them in the pool standing on two good legs: "We've found our home. My leg is healing and my fever is gone." He pointed south and proclaimed to all, even though only Buck could understand him: "Big Lick is that way beyond those woods. We can live off this land. This morning I awoke before dawn to see deer drinking water from a stream over there," he pointed. "And birds so big and fat they couldn't fly," he laughed. "We can build a shelter first, then a home. We can take the money we have to buy the seeds we need to grow our own food." Then, Ever realized that Buck was the only one who understood what he'd said and he burst into laughter. But Buck was beside himself with a new fear, since the coins were not inside his trouser pocket. Ever asked Buck what he was looking for.

"The coins must've fallen from my pocket into the water!" Buck cried out in anguish for losing something so important for their new life here. Soon Ever and James joined in the search with Dolly sitting on the bank of the springs with her feet in the warm water. While diving together and scouring the bottom for the coins, they'd surface and Ever would talk about destiny to Buck, how things like this are planned by God. Just then: Ever spotted the red berries of a mulberry tree hanging on branches on the other side of the pool and knew their hunger would be over soon. "Destiny is like seeing the world as if everything has a purpose. Like these lost coins."

"What do you mean?" Buck was crying for the loss he caused.

"Well, maybe these coins are lost so we can see what comes our way without them," Ever was trying to console the distraught lad who kept diving down to search a patch of the pool's bottom then coming up for air.

"That doesn't make sense"; Buck said, adding, "I think I lost them so I better find them."

When Ever floated Dolly over to the mulberry tree for a treat, he told her how he'd heard on The Dutchman that mulberries were good for dysentery and killing parasites. Soon, James found the coins near the bank where Buck first entered the water. James's beaming face when he showed everyone he'd found their treasure pleased Buck immensely. About this time Dolly's face and hands were covered with the delicious red berries; she started to cry, thinking she was bleeding. Ever rinsed off her hands and dropped more berries into her tiny palms, which she consumed with delight as well as James and her brother. Now, Everson Golly was seeing his family being restored by this Heaven on earth he literally fell into.

Ever had Buck wash Dolly's fine red hair and massage her scalp gently in the hotter part of the pool to kill her head lice, whereupon they all soaked their heads, since they've all had head lice since setting sail from England. Now, upon soaking for these morning hours, Dolly and the boys sat on the grass beside the pool as Ever got out of the pool and showed them how his injured leg had healed by revealing the pink color replacing the gangrene on his wound. Drying in the hot morning sun, Ever had them all sit in a circle with each boy holding one of Ever's and Dolly's hands in morning prayer. They followed their leader by bowing their heads with him.

"We thank God for our safe arrival and good fortune to find this place I hereby name Golly Springs. This will be the place on earth we call home until we are called to our home to live with you forever. Dear God, thank you for healing us here and keeping us together over our long journey. You've blessed us with health among the dying and led us here to your healing waters I name Golly Springs. We will look to you for guidance in all things. Help us see all the blessings you bestow on us.

And God, do give me the strength to provide for your children, Buck…

"Bucklin Dunn," the boy said, as if to make sure God heard his full name.

"Bucklin Dunn, Dolly Dunn, and James Virginia are the names of your children here," Ever smiled.

Ever could see that James had tears dripping down his bowed face, as if hearing his name spoken in this united circle gave him back the family he lost along with the realization that he had escaped a life of slavery because of this man Everson Golly. Yes, James Virginia already loved these white people who cared for him in this new world that was so different than the one he knew in Africa.

***

For three days they literally lived off mulberries. They'd gathered enough leafy mulberry branches to make a 7' by 7' shelter close to Golly Springs, a natural bathing area they used every day. Everson continued soaking his leg for hours every day in the hot springs that saved his life. His shark bite was turning into scar tissue and his leg as good as new while he and the boys worked tirelessly until they had a roof of branches 4 feet high above dry ground.

Their first day on this land Everson named Golly Springs, James found this fresh water creek running north to south in the forest to the west not even a couple hundred paces from their shelter in a stand of oak trees. Smiling James came back to their shelter with a full bag of water that Ever tasted first. Then, with the aid of his walking stick, with James leading the way, Ever limped over to the creek that turned east beyond the south end of the clearing. The creek was another blessing for Ever, knowing

49

now that fresh water was close enough. They could build their home in this valley that appeared to be isolated with no other homesteads for miles in any direction.

Each day, Ever regained some of his strength and used it to scout further and further each time; he was looking for roads and neighbors. He found a road on the western side over the hills named Great Road, the only road that led to Big Lick to the south and Lexington to the north. It became clear to Ever that there was no access to Golly Springs and a road had to be made south through heavy forest as well as a bridge had to be built over the creek Ever named James Creek.

On the fourth day since Ever found Golly Springs, Ever felt strong enough to make what he estimated a 5-mile walk to Big Lick straight south on Great Road. He had a list of the things he wanted to get with his money; and, he knew he'd have to look for work in Big Lick in order to build their home and support his ready-made family. After surviving his journey to this point, and while walking along without his stick along Great Road –he believed he could do anything. He had the boys leading their trek south to Big Lick with Dolly riding his right hip. He was giving the boys a sense of leadership this way; and, Ever knew that his destiny was here now and he had to trust all things coming to him on this journey and not fear what came to him. A list of a thousand things he could not afford to buy was on his mind. They had the land, plenty of fresh water, a place to bathe and rest their tired bodies, as well as enough trees to build a sturdy home that will keep them warm this winter. They needed animals to plow their land and haul timber as well as for transporting them to and from the markets in Big Lick. They'd need a good axe, food, as well as supplies and tools necessary to build a good home with a good roof.

50

In Ireland Ever had promised his father and friends he'd never sign a contract to be an indentured servant for some rich American planter, even though some 80% of the Irish men coming to the Americas were doing so. *Not for me,* Ever reminded himself while talking with the children as they walked along Great Road. He had to clear a road himself from Golly Springs south to the road that led to Lynchburg. At the back of Ever's mind he kept hearing those words spoken by that stinking driver on the wagon train, that there was work to be had in the salt wells around Big Lick. *"It's hard work and pays three dollars a week plus room and board,"* the driver barked. *"'Cept that nigger boy would never get that much from any white man 'round these parts."* Ever was thankful that James could not have understood those ugly words spoken about him. *But did he?* Ever often wondered, especially whenever they'd pass by so many images of slavery and hear the slurs cast upon those people in bondage; and then: that big ivory smile of James Virginia. It was all so mysterious to Everson Golly, how the boy could see all this slavery and poor treatment of his people and smile through it all.

In Ireland and England, slavery was recently outlawed; and yet there were plenty of indentured servants who worked for the American businessmen in the cities of the north. The poor whites with no education fared no better than the black slaves from Africa. Many slaves at least had a roof over their heads and food provided by their masters, while the poor whites worked for meagre wages, long hours, and no place to call "home". Slaves were at least valued to some degree –like animals paid for and fed in order to sustain the profits of the wealthy planters. Stories in Dublin were circulating about the Irish living in sewers and filthy shacks in American cities. That's why Ever wanted to live away from the city, on land where people were fewer and farther between. The 1840s in

Dublin had taught him that much. And his father's constant harpings about not trusting the rich Americans, reminding his son again and again: *"Claim some land in America right away – before all the wealthy buy it up. White slavery is as real as the black Africans know it's real. It's disguised better in the northern cities of America, where the slaves are the poor whites as well as every other race. America is for the rich, where slavery is still allowed and whether disguised or not. Low wages paid by the rich white man will be your master unless you stake your claim to a piece of land. Work hard son, and the land will sustain you and your family for as long as the earth provides."*

Rebecca's Garden

Not quite two miles away from Big Lick, a miracle happened. Bonham Salt Wells was owned by Irishman H. L. Bonham, the owner of the wagon train Ever and the children rode from Petersburg. Mr. Bonham was a serious man of 55 years and had no tolerance for laziness. "Boss Bonham" hired Everson soon after he walked into his busy office toting three children. *An odd mix I'd never seen the likes of: three redheads from Dublin and a slave boy.*

As Irish luck would have it, Boss Bonham, orphaned at 7, had a soft heart for orphans and truly wanted to help this young man upon hearing his tale how he inherited this ready-made family before even reaching the shores of Virginia. Mr. Bonham's proposal to Ever was incredible:

"Well Mr. Everson Golly, either you're the luckiest man alive or we both are. I've got this team of mules ready to haul fifty-pound salt bags to Lynchburg thirty miles every day, 'cept I need a driver…and a helper," the red-faced Irishman winked at Buck, a lad that reminded him of another lad about his age who came to America penniless and orphaned nearly fifty years ago. Everson caught his breath as if he'd just won the Irish Sweepstakes. Then the boss said: "I'll pay you a dollar a day. And your helper," he looked down at Buck, "a dollar a week." Buck looked over at James, who was looking down at the floor like a submissive slave. Buck put his arm around James's shoulders and said to Mr. Bonham, "What about my brother James? He can be a helper too." Bonham shifted in his chair, resisting the urge to tell this upstart Irish lad that he doesn't have a single slave on his payroll. Ever kept quiet as the boss rubbed his chin as if thinking things over. The old salt baron didn't mind having slaves digging out and bringing up salt for him in his wells because these were slaves contracted out by their owners; yet to have a "nigger" seen by the public in his salt wagons was another thing. Then, Bonham was captivated by little Dolly, her left thumb planted in her mouth while in the arms of Ever.

"Two dollars a month for your brother... but get some clothes on his back and shoes on his feet for Christ's sake," the boss pointed at James. Buck smiled and reached over the desk to shake hands on the deal, whereupon Ever did the same.

"Thank you, sir," Ever was grateful.

"Don't thank me, son; thank your dolly-pawed girl there. She's a keeper," Bonham laughed at the lass in Ever's arms that reminded him of his own daughter. "Be here at the crack of dawn tomorrow."

"Yes sir," Ever smiled and left with his family in tow.

Once outside the Bonham Salt office, not much more than a 20'x20' shack without windows, Ever walked his tribe over to the nearest shade for a drink of their water under an oak tree in front of a white little house that had a white picket fence around it. Behind the fence was a garden with various vegetables growing on vines: tomatoes, cucumbers, radishes, onions, and of course potatoes. Just then: Ever could see that James was watching two male slaves working above a salt well; they were

pulling on ropes and loading 50-lb. blocks of salt that the new
Golly crew would be delivering tomorrow in Lynchburg.

"Did we ever get lucky," Ever smiled down at Buck. "And
you, getting your brother James work, that was one good piece
of business negotiating from Bucklin Dunn."

"I'll give him a dollar a month of my wages so it's fair, but
he won't care if I do or not," Buck put his arm around his
brother's neck again.

"He'd be happy just to be with us," Ever agreed, smiling
back at James.

"Well," Ever sighed after giving Dolly a drink of water, "it's
our money and it's going to build us a fine home on Golly
Springs."

Buck nodded in agreement as Ever wiped the late morning
sun from his freckled brow while adding, "Let's get your brother
a shirt and some shoes."

"Where do we go?" Buck asked.

"Big Lick."

"Why do they call it Big Lick?" Buck was curious.

"What I heard was that the Indians called it Big Lick because
the wild game came here for the salt licks."

Two rickety wagons hauling corn and wheat passed them.
The drivers were slaves who cast a smile at James, who watched
them roll by and on their way to Big Lick. Just then: Everson
saw a young woman coming out the front door of the white
house; she was fair-skinned like Ever and wore a clean off-white
gingham dress that matched her bonnet that concealed her

55

shaded emerald green eyes. She wore a kelly-green scarf around her neck that framed her reddish-brown hair. The pail she carried clanged a bit as she was startled at the sight of the man with the little girl standing beside his leg and holding onto it as if this was her protective father. Ever stepped forward to the picket fence and asked the woman where he could buy some clothes for a lad.

The woman smiled, shielding her green eyes from the sun while pointing south on Great Road that led to Big Lick, she said, "A ways down this road is a general store that has about everything. You'll see it on your right. Not much of a selection, but they do have clothing."

"Thank you," Everson smiled and dipped his head about as much as any gentleman did around here before introducing himself.

"My name is Everson Golly."

"Rebecca Bonham," she smiled back.

Right away he told her that he and his boys were starting work tomorrow for Bonham Salt. She nodded and smiled, looking at the adorable little girl Ever picked up and held on his hip.

"Is Mr. Bonham your father?" Ever was curious.

"Yes," she answered smiling at Ever.

"You have a nice garden there Ms. Bonham."

"Thank you. I'm about to dig up a few radishes and potatoes," she politely excused herself and walked over to her garden.

"I expect I can buy some seeds for my garden at this general store!" he called to her.

She nodded yes, smiling. Buck told Ever he was hungry for anything but apples and mulberries.

***

More patience was required of Ever and Buck when James wasn't allowed inside the general store. The proprietor, a corpulent middle-aged man, had a cigar stub stuck in the corner of his tobacco juice-stained lips. The man did not care if James needed clothes, snapping at Ever, "The nigger waits outside." Ever stopped Buck from speaking his mind, knowing they had to have these things in order to work and live. So outside the store Ever had Buck remove his shoe and put his bare foot alongside one of James's bare feet, whereupon Ever could see that Buck's foot was just a bit smaller than his brother's. Since James was a wee bit taller than Buck, Ever felt he could get James shoes and a shirt that fit him by having Buck there to try them on for size.

They spent their silver coins and carried what they bought back to Golly Springs. James was the best-dressed of the foursome and caught the eye of every traveler on Great Road in his black trousers and cinnamon-colored cotton shirt. His first pair of shoes was strange to him and caused discomfort to his feet the entire trek back home. In Africa he'd never worn pants, which caused him to roll up his trouser legs half-way up his skinny calves, which Buck thought comical. Buck carried an axe, hoe, and a bag of seeds that also held four ears of corn. He had fishing line with hooks and a flint box inside a cooking pot he also carried. James carried a large blanket and a roll of canvas for their shelter. Ever, besides Dolly, carried a hunting knife in a sheath with a twenty-pound bag of potatoes; 20 feet of rope was looped over his head and tied to a coffee pot filled with beans and cakes of lye soap mixed inside a handled pot hanging from his hemp belt at his hip. And Dolly: she carried a bag of rock candy in both hands. It seemed to Ever that if Dolly was happy –the whole world was right.

This time when passing Rebecca's garden, Ever could see her watching them walk by from her open kitchen window. Like her father she was impressed with the young family and their incredible story that her father shared with her during lunch at home. She had an impulsive idea to run outside to her garden with a pail, whereupon she picked some tomatoes before hurrying out to the Great Road to catch up with the family. It was a ways past her father's office when she caught up with them and offered the pail of ripe tomatoes with a smile.

"Thank you," Ever took the pail and said he'd return it.

"No, keep it. Call it a welcome to Virginia gift," she smiled at Ever and Dolly. Then, into Ever's honest blue eyes she told him how they'd have to get animals and a wagon soon.

"Soon," Ever smiled back, alive with the flirtations he was feeling. "Can you say "thank you" to Ms. Bonham?

"Rebecca is my name," she smiled at the little girl with the bluest eyes she'd ever seen.

"Thank you, Rebecca," Dolly said with her thumb in her mouth, and so cute that Dolly and Ever laughed.

She watched them walk on the left side of the road as if they were in Ireland. *"What a charming family,"* she thought and headed back inside her house.

It was an hour walk to the spot on Great Road before they ducked east into the forest of the Blue Ridge for a quarter-mile or so until they reached the open valley of Golly Springs. While hauling these tools and provisions it became crystal clear why there was nobody living on this hidden gem beside the healing pool of water: access had not been cleared to this obscure oasis. South was the direction of any road to be cleared here, Ever could see now with their makeshift shelter in sight and the things they carried back were now giving him energy as these were the things they needed to improve their home considerably.

That evening, after working until the sun set over the western rim of Golly Springs –they now have a better canvas roof held in place with axe-splintered wood. Then: they had their best meal: trout, roasted potatoes and mountain-juicy tomatoes from Rebecca's garden. With little light remaining in the valley they bathed with soap in the healing waters. While the children played in the springs, Ever could see that his leg was close to being completely healed. He was free now to lie back against the warm stones smoothed by this bubbling-hot water and let his body float with the steam and visualize the beautiful face of that young woman with the green eyes smiling at him. His mind was seeing them together and in-love with each other here on this very sacred spot that could hold their spiritual level to a high degree, just as he had felt their connection on Great Road when she brought them that pail of tomatoes. That's when he felt their kindred spirits.

And now: opening his lazy-tired eyes, a satisfied look on his face, he could see the last shards of light hitting the purple-reds of ripe mulberries hanging in the scent of a Virginia forest that was far different than anything he had smelled or seen in Ireland or England. These were new smells of spring floral in a new world, explosions that May brings to secret places like this in the Blue Ridge. Oh how he wished he could send money for his father's passage to live here, to help raise these three children that were now making sounds that only happy, well-fed children can make when they know they are part of a family, where each one is loved and cared for by every member of the family.

And then: he knew if she was here –their home would be complete. He knew it.

Fifth Sunday

You have to admire this American family. It took Ever and Company a fortnight, or two weeks, to get used to their new work routine —which was about every waking hour of every day except when sleeping. Ever would wake at 4 in the morning, get a fire going, put the coffee on and start breakfast by slicing and roasting potatoes before waking the children. Their canvas roof managed to keep out the rain and stay in place during occasional wind gusts that would sweep down into the valley and bring this incredible blast of fresh oxygen from the mountains that was instantly invigorating.

Just like every day, Ever would take his morning soak in the healing waters he believed gave him his excellent health. His muscles would be relaxed for the bone-jarring wagon ride that was 12 hours round-trip, plus the unloading and loading of a ton of salt each way. He'd help the boys unload in Lynchburg, then load again when returning to Bonham Salt so their wagon was loaded and ready for the next day with forty 50-pound blocks of Bonham Salt.

Buck named the two mules that pulled their wagon, Tom and Katie. Sometimes Dolly would sleep right through the hour-plus walk to Bonham Salt. She'd wake up in the arms of Buck or James seated beside Ever at the reins with Tom and Katie pulling a ton of salt Lynchburg was consuming every day.

Every day, some empty wagon would stop to offer the young family a ride to Bonham Salt. Ever always refused these friendly gestures offered by men driving wagons from Charlottesville, Lexington, or northern cities like Baltimore and Philadelphia.

"No, thank you, sir! We need the exercise! We ride for twelve hours as it is every day but Sunday! But thank you kindly!" Ever would wave them by and on they would continue to Bonham Salt.

Today is Saturday, the first day of summer and another payday for Ever and his boys. Tomorrow they will rest and play as their preacher encourages his flock. This will be the fifth Sunday in a row the Golly Springs family made the walk to the church in Big Lick. They will once again sit with their boss and his beautiful daughter Rebecca; then after the service they will all meet for coffee and dessert in the church basement. After this fellowship with their new neighbors they will ride in the black yellow-fringed Bonham carriage to the general store where Ever will buy his supplies needed to continue building up his homestead. Last Sunday, Ever bought a saw and was already sawing axe-felled trees into the logs that would be the four walls of their home, hopefully before winter. Saturday is the day Rebecca would be in her father's office because she was in charge of payroll. At the breakfast table this Saturday morning, before Ever and his kids arrived to drive her father's wagon to Lynchburg –she made it clear to her loving father that she liked Everson Golly: *"You know, Daddy,"* she drawled, *"Everson is such a nice young man. I see him walking down that road with those children, toting all those supplies after church and all. Can't you help him get a road cleared to his homestead?"* Her father listened, dabbed grits and bacon from his lips with Rebecca's embroidered napkins, before saying, *"I talked to him about clearing a road south through Big Gap. That's when he reminded me there's a forest to deal with, as well as a twenty-foot stream to cover for crossing."*

"Daddy, tomorrow after church we can take them from the general store to their home and see the place for ourselves."

***

All day Saturday on their round-trip drive to Lynchburg, Everson kept thinking about seeing Rebecca in church and inviting her out to Golly Springs. But then his mind would remind him that his home was but a foundation with a rough, unfinished oak floor and support beams. He couldn't be certain if she liked him for a beau; nevertheless he welcomed his daydreams about her, if only because her image gave his mind rest from his relentless goal to have their home finished before winter hit western Virginia.

In summer, after the walk home from work, there was only two hours left of light to work on the house before the setting sun would dip below the western hills and cast an ever-darkening green shadow over the valley. This is the time of day Ever wants Rebecca to be here, to show her the beauty of Golly Springs.

Before darkness came, the boys would prepare the evening meal, and getting quite good at it to Ever's delight. They'd sit at a table Ever and the boys made themselves that was a bit wobbly, especially the chairs, which they planned to level when the house was ready for winter. The boys were getting good at finding the right-sized tree and axing it down before sawing it into the logs that would secure their solid home into a cozy environment that Ever craved more than anything. For Ever was a clean-cut, fussy guy compared to most homesteaders around this part of Virginia. The work unloading and loading two tons of salt blocks a day was making them strong, each of them packing on ten or more pounds of muscle since moving here. Dolly had even gained a little weight and was talking up a storm since Rebecca started reading to Dolly and a handful of other children during Sunday services. The little redhead became known as Dolly Golly with the other children, since all their parents knew of the handsome Everson Golly, a new neighbor liked by all and known by all to be fond of Boss Bonham's daughter.

By now everyone knew the Everson Golly story: how the Irish kids lost their mother to "the fever"; and how the black slave boy named James Virginia was rescued by Everson and The Dutchman's crew during their terrible voyage to America. When Everson explained the whole ordeal to Rebecca –that's when she first knew she was in-love with Everson Golly: *"Rebecca, to tell you the honest-to-God truth, it was the children who saved me. If not for them I doubt I would've survived."*

***

On this fifth Sunday in a row, before church, on this early summer morning, Boss Bonham sat waiting on his surrey-fringed carriage holding the reins of his Palomino mare, Goldie, when Rebecca came out of the house carrying two mulberry pies she made from mulberries Ever gave her. It was starting to rain lightly. Mr. Bonham appeared to be thinking about something.

"What are you thinking about?" she asked her father.

"I'm thinking about heading north on Great Road to pick up the Golly clan."

Her big smile gave him the sign he needed and Goldie began her loping walk up the muddy road that was clear of traffic on Sunday morning. Soon, they came upon the family just when the rain increased. The boss told them to get in. They did

64

gladly. When Bonham got Goldie turned around and headed south on Great Road Rebecca gave Dolly a red and gold silk scarf. Dolly, on Ever's lap, her left thumb stuck in her mouth, smiled at Rebecca. Ever wrapped the scarf over Dolly's damp red hair, tying it under her chin, whereupon Rebecca complimented how nice it looks on her.

The boys were all too happy to be out of the rain, since first light they were up and helping Ever hoist the roof's frame into position from two 12-foot ladders each boy hammered together for this particular job. Every Saturday after getting paid by Rebecca, Ever and his tribe made their weekly trip to Mr. Heath's general store. Ever would ask the man what he needed to do next and what he'd need to do the job right. Mr. Heath, hearing that Mr. Golly was a good employee for Bonham Salt, let Ever put supplies on credit. At first, stubborn Ever resisted the offer, until Heath told the young man that only good men with steady jobs get credit in his store. And: James was now welcome in his store, having apologized to Ever for being rude when they first met.

It was on their carriage ride back from church, on this fifth Sunday in a row of going to church, that Boss Bonham continued driving Goldie on past his house toward Golly Springs. Dolly sat between Ever and Rebecca on the back seat while the boys rode up front with Mr. Bonham. Not too far along and Bonham pulled Goldie over to a pasture, pointing out the best route for access to Golly Springs through the pelting rain he roared his words to Ever:

"If you'd start clearing that ground just north of that stream and plant rice paddies, you'll have plenty of water and ducks will come! Ducks love rice! You'd have two products in big demand that you can sell to the markets in Big Lick, especially when the railroad comes through here! And it will! Then, you'll be serving duck under glass with rice to every big wig in Richmond and Washington!"

That sounded like a great idea, yet Ever had never fired a musket or pistol in his entire life. During this ride on Great Road is when Mr. Bonham made Ever an incredible offer: "I got an old mule and wagon you can have to clear that south passage. Some well-placed timber can bridge that stream. In time you could make a decent passage for a wagon and have good access."

The boss pulled Goldie over to the trail Ever pointed out, the spot where they would walk to Golly Springs. It was obvious to Rebecca that Ever tried not to sound ungrateful when he told his boss he's been spending every spare minute working to get the house ready by winter, and there was no time to clear a road to Golly Springs.

Rebecca could see that her father was really pondering Ever's situation, all the way through the woods in a slight drizzle. She also recalled her father telling someone in the office that this land was a fertile, hidden gem of a place that only needed a road to it. When the valley appeared to them, Rebecca proclaimed its beauty as her father wheezed and caught his breath in agreement. Ever pointed out the garden that was three times the size of the Bonham garden and coming along well for late planting. Beyond the skeleton frame of the house Ever pointed to the sacred steaming waters that saved his life. From here Bonham could see clearly how a wagon and animal were needed to clear a road out of this place. Ever pointed to the north woods behind the house and explained how they were able to use those trees for easiest transport. Rebecca took Dolly from Ever and carried her to the house while her father proceeded to tell Ever what he should do: "You got to have a horse or mule in here and start clearing that land to the south. Build a shelter for an animal. Hell, there's enough good pasture here to feed a herd of horses. I got this wagon you could strip down to the wheels, haul it here in a wagon, you and the boys carry it down here, put it together, and you're in business, Mr. Golly. You could clear that road, bridge a stream, and build your house smartly, saving you a bunch of time and work."

"I don't know how I'd pay you back Mr. Bonham. Everything we make goes into putting that house together and buying the things we need to live on."

"I got this old chestnut mare, she's got about two years to go before she stops working. You'd be doing me a favor to take her and I'll throw in that old wagon just to get that old mare out of my sight."

Seeing Rebecca standing with Dolly in the center of their unfinished home with the boys hanging on her every word –Ever knew this was the woman he'd marry and share their lives together. Although there were but a few rafters for the roof pegged and slotted in place as rain fell and soaked into the unfinished floor, the Bonham's could see that their work had progressed remarkably considering they were so young and living hand-to-mouth without any wagon or animal or manpower to assist them.

"This could be a fine home, couldn't it, Father?"

Bonham nodded in agreement, the old smile lines around his eyes visible and obvious to his daughter under his brown calf-skin slouchy hat. They all followed Rebecca's gaze wherever it went, until it stayed on their temporary shelter. She wanted to see the inside of this place that resembled some of the miner's living quarters she'd seen many times in the mountains. There was no door on the shelter, only a tapered oval-shaped entrance with no windows. Ever suddenly felt embarrassed when

67

Rebecca put Dolly on her feet and they went inside the shelter hand-in-hand.

Inside the shelter she saw four bundles of ragged bedding rolled up and piled against one side where slits of daylight were visible from top to bottom in their temporary sleeping area. The dirt floor was worn grass mashed to a green-black color that was cold to her touch upon kneeling to touch it. Nails held up rags of clothing on one side above cakes of lye soap placed on a piece of cut wood that was used for bathing and washing clothing. She saw a flint box and a partially used candle standing in a notched-out block of wood, a thing her father also did from his days in Ireland. Rebecca started to cry upon seeing little Dolly so innocent and oblivious to living this way.

Outside the shelter she put Dolly down to the ground and they walked over to the rock-circled fire pit where a black kettle hung over the ashes from an early-morning fire. Rebecca knelt down to Dolly as the boys came over and listened to Rebecca talk directly into the little girl's fire-blue eyes that were framed by the tangled fine red hair now covered by the red and gold silk scarf she'd given her.

"Dolly, would you like to go to school every day at my house when Ever and the boys are at work?"

The girl's eyes were not sure what "school" meant, so Rebecca used her hands to demonstrate reading and writing. Dolly's excited nod yes was all Rebecca needed to see. They went hand-in-hand over to Ever and Mr. Bonham talking near the bank of the healing waters while the boys were nearby digging for worms in the earth so they could go fishing in James Creek that ran along the west and south borders of Golly Springs. Ever was telling his boss how the water here saved their lives. That's when Mr. Bonham told Ever about the healing springs fifty miles north of here near Lexington, and how he goes there every winter for his arthritis.

"You could come here instead," Ever said to his boss with the enthusiasm of a man not quite twenty years old.

Rebecca didn't have to convince Ever that Dolly could spend each day with her learning to read and write instead of that awful bone-jarring round-trip wagon run to Lynchburg six days a week. When she suggested that the boys would do well for themselves if they went to school in Big Lick to learn how to read and write, Ever's answer was a different response:

"No, the boys will work until we're settled."

On the ride home in the Bonham carriage the boss was certain that he'd just left the homestead of his future son-in-law, and that he would soon be the grandfather of a ready-made batch of children he'd never seen the likes of in his entire life. The reports from Lynchburg were good, that Ever and the boys were good workers and well-liked by all.

Ever and Buck could tell that every work day James was confused by the appearance and treatment of slaves working for Bonham Salt at the receiving depot in Lynchburg, as well as the African men, women, and children who walked the Lynchburg Road and worked from dusk to dawn in the tobacco fields on both sides of the road for as far as the eye could see.

All that next week Dolly spent each day with her new teacher Rebecca; consequently Ever was able to pay more attention to the boys and see how they were indeed missing an education while working with him, and eventually he wanted them to learn how to read and write because he knew how important it was in order to get along in this world. In Dublin, Ever's father made sure his son was able to read and write and

69

do basic math. In Ireland, except for the worst of the poor, Ever knew well this inherent desire for Irish children to read the words and stories written by Irish writers. So, sedulous Everson Golly hatched a plan to teach the boys to read while on their long daily ride to Lynchburg and back –without hurting their income. Rebecca would help him with his plan. But not tonight, for Mr. Bonham kept his word and had his old chestnut mare, Hazel, harnessed and hitched to a wagon, ready to pull a completely disassembled wagon, wheels and all, loaded inside a Bonham Salt wagon.

Two adult male slaves, contracted by a local planter to work for Bonham Salt, rode with the wagon parts and tools while Ever and family rode up front. Another contracted slave was already leading another old horse to northern edge of Big Gap where Hazel would be unhitched from the wagon and led by Buck to Golly Springs, whereupon the other horse would pull the wagon further north up Great Road to the west hills where all would unload the wagon parts, carry them to Golly Springs and assemble it right away.

Before night fell, Everson Golly had an assembled wagon with a harnessed, experienced animal ready to help him clear the south woods to Big Gap that Mr. Bonham knew would speed up the Golly home construction.

By the end of the work week, Saturday, the boys managed to clear enough trees to begin the road that would afford access to the world of trade and travel. They cleared and sawed more than enough wood to build Hazel a 3-sided shelter with the open side facing the north woods, keeping snow drifts to a minimum, another Boss Bonham suggestion.

Every evening after work, the boys could hitch Hazel to the wagon, head south, and pick up where they'd left off, clearing a trail of timber they could then haul back to saw for finishing the roof on their home. Ever estimated they had maybe 150 days or five months to get their home built before winter. The boys and Ever were all twenty pounds heavier, solid muscle, and more confident about reaching their incredible goal.

"We'll do it!" Ever would call out to the boys, "And we'll have a bridge crossing James Creek to boot!"

Then James or Ever would spell "boot" out loud to each other, whether riding on the wagon or clearing timber. The boys admired Ever's plan for their education that he had put into action ever since that fifth Sunday when Rebecca began teaching Dolly the alphabet at a vigorous rate. Rebecca's positive reports on Dolly's progress gave hope to Ever that their rough voyage had somehow hurt her capacity of speech. Rebecca assured Ever that Dolly was going to do very well for herself.

Learners and Earners

Rebecca Bonham helped create and paid for all six copies of the rudimentary *"Alphabet and Vowel Book,"* a cloth-bound parchment paper edition sewn together and hand-printed by ladies Rebecca knew from church. One of those first copies went to Ever, who put it to good use right away by teaching the boys their alphabet on their ride to Lynchburg and back. While one of the boys held the reins on their robotic route, Ever would go through the entire alphabet with the other boy. It was fun for all of them, and quite amusing to Ever that James was catching on faster than Buck, thus igniting a healthy competition between them that would keep them interested in learning.

Every sunrise, well on their way to Lynchburg, Ever was thrilled to hold the open book and say out loud the letter then the vowel of the word. Even reticent James was coming out of his shell and speaking out the sounds with vibrant clarity, all the while competing with the steady, clomping thud of the Bonham mule team mixed with constant sounds of moving wheels making their rickety clatter over a 5-hour stretch of earth-worn Virginia dirt and mud.

Then, with an empty wagon for the return ride at the same speed, James would take hold of the reins and Buck would out-shout the letter and word above his quieter brother, causing James to laugh and giggle. Sometimes Ever would take the reins and he'd have the boys repeat their lesson together with James encouraged to be louder and louder as occasional pedestrians and black and white indentured servants and slaves in the fields would look to see the source of this schooling coming from the moving Bonham Salt wagon.

Meanwhile in Rebecca's cozy parlor at home, she and Dolly would be going through the same alphabet book with three other girls not much older than Dolly; their mothers were there to help their children learn to read and write. Dolly Dunn was the quietest and most withdrawn of the children, and yet she was making progress and excited to be in this all-female environment versus the all-male influence at Golly Springs. This maternal balance for Dolly pleased Ever too, for he'd seen many a lass back home develop into "toughs" if they lived among males for most of their early years. He uttered sincere words to Rebecca that first time he left Dolly with her:

"I appreciate this good work you do with the children. I know in my heart that it's best for Dolly to spend time in your good hands."

That one heartfelt compliment from Everson Golly tore into Rebecca Bonham's heart and remained there as a favorite memory for all time.

***

Day by day the back-straining clearing of a road south from Golly Springs continued. The felling and hauling of timber, the measuring and sawing; all of this persistent work done after the day's work for Bonham Salt was leading to winning the race against the coming winter.

James was displaying more confidence, and Buck was doing his best to match his brother's enthusiasm for learning, especially when Rebecca gave them another book, this one with sentences, another book she created for the children titled *"Learners and Earners."* Ever and the boys managed to learn while they were at work and started using their growing vocabulary to figure out ways to make Bonham Salt more efficient and thus profitable. A "gem" of an idea came to Ever when he and the boys were unloading their load of block salt at The General Store in Lynchburg. Ever knew that a 50-lb. block of salt could be ground for table consumption and sold to the public in 5-lb. sacks that generated more money per pound for both the wholesaler and retailer. Since most of their salt blocks were sold to customers for their animals, Ever found out that these same customers shaved and ground their salt supply for their own kitchen supply from these blocks of salt.

When Ever told his boss about this idea there was one big hitch: What material or container would be used to hold these 5-lb. sacks of already-ground salt? Ever's answer pleased his boss:

"We'd deliver it ground up in barrels. Each customer would bring their own sack and scoop out salt by the pound."

The boss was happy with this business idea, not because he'd never thought of it, but rather; now he had a man who was courting his only child, a man who had the energy to force Bonham Salt to support a family he hoped to have before he died. After some thinking on it:

"Alright Mr. Everson Golly, I'll supply the barrel, grind the salt, and you get Lynchburg's general store to buy a barrel. You deliver it and I'll split the profit with you."

Ever's freckled, calloused right hand extended across Bonham's desk: "You got yourself a deal, Mr. Bonham."

They left Bonham's office knowing this meant more money for them and happily walked to the Bonham house to get Dolly. Dolly burst out the front door wearing a white cotton dress and carrying 3 pair of underwear, all sewn by her teacher for her favorite student. Ever was impressed with Dolly's new outfit and hair that Rebecca trimmed and styled in a ponytail with a purple ribbon made of lace, both Dolly and Rebecca's favorite color. "Don't you look pretty, Miss Dolly Dunn," Ever smiled down at the happy girl who now insisted on walking everywhere –like the other girls. The boys stood behind Ever, looking at their sister's new look when Rebecca came outside in her apron, her reddish-brown hair pinned back. She looked so beautiful to Ever. She handed Dolly a cake of rose-scented bath soap wrapped in a gauzy cloth.

"What do you say to Rebecca?" Ever asked the girl with a sparkle in her blue eyes.

"Thank you," Dolly smiled.

"And what else?" Ever asked.

"See you tomorrow," Dolly waved goodbye.

"See you tomorrow," Rebecca smiled and walked with them to the fence and asked Ever how the road through South Gap was coming along.

"We'll have the bridge finished soon. Once that's done there won't be that much clearing to do."

"Good," Rebecca smiled and nodded and watched the family walk north along Great Road, all the while wishing she was going with them, for she admired them so much for the life they had together.

During this walk home in early July, Dolly noticed that they left Great Road and were going a different way to get home, through a forest of mixed oak and pine. They spooked deer and fluttering wild turkeys scampering into deep grass behind shrubs and hemlock. Ever's keen eye for topography could see the best possible route for this final stretch of road that would be cleared soon and open their world at Golly Springs.

The boys ran ahead of Ever and Dolly, wanting to walk over the logs they had placed across the stream at its narrowest spot, each boy wanting to be the first to take this long-awaited shortcut that will save them half their walking time to work and back. In their haste to be the first over this crossing - the boys ran through a thicket of poison ivy, ignoring Ever's warning weeks ago when first clearing land for their new home: *"Leaves of three: leave them be."*

Upon seeing the boys grimacing from the stinging nettles and scratching their arms and legs where the nettles pierced their pants, Ever told them to go soak in Golly Springs, "clothes and all!" The boys heeded his advice and high-tailed it to the springs with James being the faster of the two.

By the time Ever and Dolly reached the springs, the boys were contentedly soaking in the healing waters that already had healed their injuries from poison ivy. Soon, the boys had their wet clothes hanging out to dry after changing and riding Hazel out to do more clearing of the access road while Ever prepared the evening meal with Dolly helping. By the time the boys returned home after sunset with a load of timbre for the house – Ever and his helper had a healthy supper of trout and potatoes with the first sweet corn of the season.

After feeding and watering Hazel, the boys carried their dirty dishes to the western part of James Stream to clean them after every meal. Kneeling at the rushing stream it was James who saw that they were being watched. At this point James did not know the name of indigenous people that the white man called "*Indians.*" The African boy had never seen an Indian before and warned Buck, "Men watch us." Buck followed his brother's relaxed eyes to the three young male Indians standing still in the woods on the western slope watching these white and black men like curious deer. Buck stood up and waved at them; and, like deer –they scampered deeper into the woods on soundless feet.

***

It was apparent to Ever that Rebecca would be his future wife, for she talked more and more about her father's early life as if she wanted Ever to know she too had been raised by a good man. She told Ever how her father brought her here from Belfast 16 years ago after her mother died from "the fever." Her father discovered and dug out a profitable salt mine in the western hills of the Blue Ridge behind their present-day home. This kind of salt came from a rich vein of gypsum that's pink in color and used for salt lick for cattle and horses that require high mineral content, especially for the horses during the summer months. Young Bonham taught himself how to shape the pink salt into 50-lb. blocks for animals. Bonham's salt blocks were well received because they were not as hard as other salt blocks. Cattle have rough tongues and have no trouble licking the salt from the blocks; however, horses tongues aren't nearly as rough as cattle and consequently end up biting into the blocks to get their salt needs met, causing injuries to the horse's jaw. Ever was aware that Bonham Salt has a good reputation with farmers, ranchers and planters, providing them with a good product for their horses.

Day after day on Ever's run to Lynchburg, he was now a thinking businessman, not just a wage earner. He started raking up a few pellets of pink salt that had fallen onto the wagon's bed and he and the boys would suck on them during these hottest of summer's days, getting not as fatigued as before. Ever began handing these gem-shaped crystals out to the slave children and workers he could get to in the field. He called them "Bonham Salt Rocks." The boys enjoyed seeing Ever drop a fistful of "rocks" into the apron of a woman slave after showing her the pink salt rock on his tongue. As time went on, the people would watch for Ever, run to his wagon, get some salt rocks and run back into the field.

Rebecca's off-white pieces of cloth she'd use to wrap bars of soap and little gifts with a tiny pink ribbon - gave Ever the idea to call his product Bonham Salt Gems. Ever would spend hours brainstorming with Rebecca each week how he could first sell the farmers, ranchers, and planters the gems to give to their slaves and indentured servants in the hot Virginia fields. He'd tell these men that these people need the minerals as much as animals, and how much that would benefit the health of his workers and their production. He would tell them they would work with more energy. Buck was the one to nail down the price of these "gems": "Put the same amount in a bag, sell it for ten times what it cost you."

"Why ten times?" Ever was curious.

"Boss Bonham says so. He knows."

So, when they had their product bagged and tied with a pink ribbon, a color that the boss liked because of his pink salt, Ever, Rebecca, and the three kids watched intently as Boss Bonham poured the pink gems onto a scale, made notations, and sat back pondering the figures while they waited anxiously for good news.

"You'll have to sell something to these people they don't think they need," Bonham said.

The young Irishman's answer surprised his boss: "Saltville, Virginia, supplies all the granulated salt for every kitchen in Virginia, North Carolina and Tennessee, right?"

The boss gave his positive nod.

"Fieldworkers get their salt from their food, no place else. They lose all their salt from sweatin' all day in the sun. I can sell small amounts to a new customer coming and going every day. Once they see the "gems" in a barrel at the general store –they'll buy what they want."

Between and during notations the boss talked about the numbers to Ever:

"There's about thirty gems to a four-ounce bag. There's the crushing of blocks…"

"A tap of the hammer," Ever smiled.

"We'd have to get at least twenty cents a pound," Bonham figured, then a wink at little "Dolly Blue Eyes".

"I can sell it to the planter and the store, convince both there's a real need to keep their workers healthy like their animals," Ever claimed with such enthusiastic confidence that the boss could not resist. They shook on splitting the sales of the new product evenly, and so a partnership was begun.

First and Last Christmas Together

Ever and his little clan had a roof over their heads by late October. The interior of their 30' x 30' home had a ways to go before being finished. A rock chimney fireplace was keeping them warm, cooking the meals, drying their clothes, and markedly improving the quality of their lives. None of them had a bed yet; however, they made two bed stands way in advance of purchasing their first mattress, planning to buy one at a time and sharing it. The boys would share it with Dolly one night and Ever the next night until they saved enough money to get their second mattress. Both beds would end up stowed during the day and used on the open unfinished main room at night until they finished the three small bedrooms.

Ever was relieved to have a good roof over their heads before winter came to their little valley. The South Road was finished and now they had Hazel pull them to work and back six days a week, and to church and the store and back on Sundays. The boys got so they preferred walking alongside the rough wagon ride along their new access road, a trip that was anything but smooth, especially over the James Stream Bridge that was incredibly bumpy and jostling to any passengers when the front wheels first landed and when leaving it. Ever thought the wagon was going to fall apart at every crossing, so he had the kids walk across after he drove the wagon over alone.

Since the colder fall weather, James had to wear shoes all the time. He didn't like wearing the stiff leather shoes that made his feet hurt whenever he wore them. Two weeks ago they were all given their first winter coats, a gift from the church brethren. Rebecca made Dolly's gray, goose-down hooded winter coat along with matching mittens and wool scarf. Ever and the boys received gray fleece coats with wool caps and gloves made by these church women who were sewing, baking, and preserving year-round just to keep their flock comfortable. Ever's coat was given to him by a recent widow who wanted to give the young man who sat in front of her with his family every Sunday a nice gift for the coming winter now upon them.

Ever put in lots of extra time and energy into his "gem" of an idea he'd pitched to dozens of planters and "businessmen" between Golly Springs and Lynchburg. He sold some bags of salt gems here and there, the pink ribbon-tied cloth bags not catching on, with sales petering out after the cold weather hit. Every day on their run to Lynchburg, slaves and indentured servants (mostly Irishmen) would stand by the road waiting for the Bonham Salt wagon, whereupon Ever and the boys would stop, scoop up loose gems on the wagon bed and hand them out. No wagon driver was more popular than Everson Golly, known by all as the *"Salt and Pepper Man"* because of the black boy always with him who Ever referred to as *"my son, James."*

Fall exploded all at once around Golly Springs their first October, when every tree seemed to be any color but green. It was on one of those glorious inchoate October Sunday mornings, when the wagon ride to church on South Gap Road led to the expression of love Ever and Rebecca could not conceal any longer. Every Sunday Ever was stopping his wagon alongside the fringe-covered Bonham carriage that was waiting in front of

81

the Bonham house. Dolly liked to ride to church with her teacher, so she rode with Rebecca and her father.

As every Sunday was getting colder, James was feeling more and more the effects of winter on his African-acclimated body, shivering like a new-born pup until well into the minister's sermon. *"One thing about James,"* Buck said discreetly to Ever, *"he may get so cold his teeth chatter, but he never complains, never."*

Of late, after church, Dolly stayed with Rebecca helping her teacher in the church basement serving coffee and sweets and cleaning up afterwards. Today, *"Doll,"* the nickname Herb Bonham gave Dolly, would ride back to the Bonham house in the carriage, and she'd stay there until Ever and the boys stopped to get her after picking up their ordered feather mattress at the general store.

When Ever and his helpers arrived with their new mattress loaded on the wagon, Rebecca came outside with Dolly carrying an armload of beige-colored curtains she'd made for their bare shuttered windows she'd measured weeks ago when she and her father were invited to dinner when their house finally had a door, four walls, and a roof over it. At dinner Ever formally named their new home Golly Springs during a toast at their table on wobbly chairs Rebecca found *"adorable."* Ever really liked Mr. Bonham's democratic idea to put the naming of the house to a vote. Golly Springs was the unanimous choice. The boss then leaned over to Dolly and told her his choice would be to name the new house *"Dolly Springs."* Rebecca wanted her father to make a toast, and so with raised glasses all-around the table the boss toasted: *"To Golly Springs, may it be a solid home blessed by God."*

***

It was no surprise to Mr. Bonham that Everson Golly asked him for Rebecca's hand in marriage right after a late November dinner at the Bonham house. The boss gave his approval with a firm handshake and big hug, all from a man who never showed his feelings to anyone except his daughter. Rebecca and Ever spent every day together after their engagement, with a wedding date of next Easter Sunday. The boss insisted that Rebecca's dowry be that Everson came into his salt business as a partner. *"Bonham & Golly,"* Ever suggested with a grin. To Ever's surprise, the boss agreed to the new business name. Herb Bonham wanted very much to keep his only child and ready-made grandchildren close to him in a young and growing country like 1847 America.

Those colder and colder days until Christmas, every work day afternoon, Rebecca would drive Dolly in the carriage to Golly Springs. Almost every day she would bring along some new item she bought or created for her new home. The teacher and student would have supper ready for the "men," who never failed to look so forward to returning home as now. Like her fiancé, Rebecca Bonham wanted all things in order by her wedding day.

Luckily, snowfall was not extreme until Christmas Eve, when a foot of snow fell fast in *"flakes the size of pearls,"* Rebecca wrote in her diary Christmas Eve, forcing the Bonhams to spend the night at Golly Springs after a fantastic Christmas Eve dinner of goose, yams and potatoes, cranberries, sweet bread, with pumpkin pie for dessert.

Rebecca's frugal, homespun taste, along with her desire to make a comfortable home was so apparent to her father, for the holiday smells around Golly Springs reminded him of their own home. Ever and the boys had finished the bedrooms, and thanks to Rebecca –three more mattresses for each of the children.

That freezing Christmas Eve evening six stockings were hanging from the mantel above the roaring fire as Herb sipped his favorite blackberry brandy and five voices sang Christmas carols from 2 homemade songbooks Rebecca put together for this occasion. James and Buck shared one of the books while seated in front of the fire on a black bear rug Rebecca brought from home. Dolly sang along, having memorized every song with her teacher, in order to have these cherished moments their first Christmas at Golly Springs. All were having a grand time while blowing, drifting snow silently piled high against the solid oak door that earlier Mr. Bonham had admired considering the novice carpenters involved.

That night, Ever and the boys slept together on the black bear rug before the fire, giving up their beds to company. Dolly slept in her bed in her little room next to the master bedroom, where she could hear the boss snoring away after his big meal and brandy. Even the boys made fun of the old man's snoring and began giggling when Ever covered his ears to feign the obnoxiousness of their sleeping employer and future grandfather. Sleep would not come for Ever and Rebecca, for earlier they secretly planned to meet at the dining table when all the children were asleep. There were gifts to fill the stockings, precious things that would surely be buried in snow by now in the carriage parked outside the door.

Not long after hearing the sounds of sleep coming from both boys, Ever got up to stoke the fire before dressing and heading out in a foot of snow to check on the animals. It wasn't terribly cold since the wind died down; the horses stood together sleeping, their wet nostrils snorting clouds of air. They awoke when Ever broke up the ice in the water buckets hanging in a corner of the 3-sided shelter. For a few moments he turned and looked at his roof on his home that was covered by the first deep blanket of winter. He breathed in the sweet smells of horses and fresh hay and relaxed his eyes in the blue smoke that rose from the chimney skyward and vanished quickly into the ink-black night of stars, some brighter than others and twinkling like the stars he'd seen when crossing the great ocean. Because it was Christmas Eve he was feeling most blessed. He thought of how he wished his father could be here to live in the home he already was planning to expand. He kept thinking about his father on his way back to the house while following his snow holes; it was strange that his life in Dublin had been another life that was gone forever. He told Rebecca, *"It's as if my father died. Because I know I'll never see him again."* Then: he could see the rising steam from the springs, and so made a new path to the sacred water that he knew had saved his life.

Not long ago he was surrounded by abject poverty in dark Dublin; now he stood in snow looking out to the edge of a mystery pool of boiling water and steam that had this miracle power to heal a dying man. Thanks to this water he had three children and a good woman he would marry and make a home here, a safe haven to raise his family. He heard the front door open behind him and saw Rebecca smiling and bundled in a full-length fox fur coat, her head covered with a maroon-colored shawl. She made her way to him in the snow laughing like a happy woman. They kissed and laughed and he swept away a piece of ground to place his clothes as he started to remove his clothes.

"Everson Golly, what are you doing?" she whispered. She watched him ease into the bubbling water she'd heard so much about.

'I'm going in, and I hope you join me," he laughed.

She looked back at the house and knew her father slept sound every night until five every morning. Then, she turned back to the man she loved, who stood in the waist-high steaming water holding out his strong arms for her to join him. Quickly she removed her clothes, piling them on his clothes, whereupon she gingerly stepped to the pool's edge and fell into his waiting arms, both laughing with joy in the healing hot springs. She resisted playing and splashing, for not wanting to get her hair wet before returning to the house as Ever swam completely submerged and moved further away from the heat source into the cooler water that was incredibly invigorating. Soon, he pulled her out to the deeper, colder water; now she was feeling never so free in her life, further and further away from the guilt of sin and the fear of God's punishment. They both hurried back to the warmer water by its source, all the while laughing and playing and knowing they had done nothing wrong that needed forgiveness from God or any man.

They leaned their backs against the worn-smooth rocks protruding from the bank and kissed in the rising steam of this sparkling miracle water after wishes of *"Merry Christmas,"* their bodies obscured and free from human judgments. That was as far as things would go, for Rebecca whispered to him that she was *"not about to wear any color but white on my wedding day."*

Ever respected and needed the sensibilities of a strong woman like Rebecca Bonham. They laughed and enjoyed the healing waters for some time before getting dressed quickly. Upon bringing in the gifts from the carriage Ever discovered his gift from his boss and future father-in-law. An 1840 flintrock musket was wrapped inside a Cherokee floor rug that Rebecca and her father bought in Big Lick for the Golly family.

Inside the warm house again, the happiest of couples filling the stockings on the mantel quietly, that's when Herb Bonham left this one place on earth where his daughter would hopefully spend the rest of her life.

***

The death of Herb Bonham was nothing close to a surprise for his daughter because of the numerous seizures her father had over the last few years. Before, his seizures were in the morning before heading off to his office or to church. Rebecca told Ever that *"It was as if the energy it took to start his day took too much out of him."*

Something else warned Rebecca of her father's passing: he never failed to get up early, always the first one to get a roaring fire going and a fresh pot of coffee. She feared something was wrong when the playful sounds of joy had not aroused him from the bedroom. Each child was going over each gift and sharing it right away, letting the others hold it if they wanted. There were winter stockings for all; gloves and scarves knitted and dyed by Rebecca; and each of the large stockings held a tightly rolled pair of long underwear bottoms; topped off by peppermint candy canes she made hanging over the top of every stocking. Amidst the noise of inchoate joy made by Ever and the children –that's when Rebecca had waited long enough and went into Ever's bedroom to find that her father had died peacefully in his sleep. She saw right away that he was gone and asked Ever to come into his room. That's when she broke down crying, when telling Ever her father had passed away during the night. Her loss was tempered by not wanting to alarm the children and ruin their Christmas morning. Ever assured her that the children had seen plenty of death on their voyage to America, and that her father's passing should not be withheld from them.

87

Ever left Rebecca alone with her father and told the children that Mr. Bonham had passed away last night, explaining that their boss wanted to leave this earth and be with God on Christmas Day. Rebecca came out of Ever's room after the children were told. She was surprised how calm and steady they were, showing her their amazing strength considering their youth.

"May we say goodbye to him?" Buck asked Rebecca.

"Of course you may," she cried into her handkerchief.

Ever and Rebecca stood holding hands behind the children as Buck, James, then Dolly said their goodbyes to the man that had been so good to them. Then, the children left the room. Rebecca thought they should put her father in the carriage in order to preserve the body for Mr. Roth the local undertaker and a member of their church.

"The carriage is too small. I'll have Hazel pull the salt wagon closer to the door and he can stay there until we can get out of here tomorrow, I hope."

"He should be covered," she cried into Ever's chest.

Now: James was thinking about his parents, wondering if he'd ever see them again. Looking into the light of his brother's brown eyes, Buck said to his brother, "Do you think he knew he was dying?"

James shrugged and said, "Only God knows."

"Do you think Rebecca knew her father was dying?" James asked his brother.

"I don't know. Why don't you ask her," Buck said.

"Ask me what?" Rebecca surprised the boys.

James was embarrassed, and more so when Buck said, "James wanted to know if you knew that your father was dying?"

"I knew there was something wrong, because he was having trouble sleeping; and he'd have these times when he'd shake all over, like something was seriously wrong. My father was a stubborn man and made light of it no matter how much I begged him to see a doctor."

"Does this mean we don't work for Bonham Salt anymore?" Buck asked Rebecca.

"Oh, yes, you will all work just the same. The business is mine now. And certainly all of you can work at Bonham Salt as long as you want."

"You are the boss now?" James asked.

"Yes, James, I am your boss now," she smiled then covered her trembling mouth from shock and grief upon losing the man who had raised her alone.

Rebecca watched Ever and the boys carry her father's covered body outside to the wagon parked near the door. Seeing how careful and respectful they were, especially sweet smiling James, made her detest slavery all the more as her father had. And yet: her father supported the insidious institution that England abolished several years earlier. She believed that this hypocrisy was a part of his early death, and told Ever of this later when alone. Doing payroll for Bonham Salt she saw that her father paid the slaveholders one dollar per week for each slave's hard labor in the salt wells and mines that Bonham Salt owned. Rebecca also knew from the company records she kept that her father made a small fortune off slave labor. She confessed to her fiancé that without those low slave labor costs, *"we'd be living not much better than the slaves themselves, since that was how we were able to keep our prices competitive."* Rebecca was so certain in her plaintive tone that slavery had played a part in her father's death, that Ever could never question its validity.

***

It was a few days after Mr. Bonham's funeral service in church that Ever confessed to his bride-to-be that he could no longer work for Bonham Salt if slaves were contracted out by slaveholders. There was no mention of James by Ever, and needn't be mentioned anyway, for not only did Rebecca abhor slavery –she wasn't about to profit from it and live in the same heart-wrenching guilt her father carried with him. There was an "economic leverage problem" to overcome regarding this insidious way of life that the southern states were addicted to. That's exactly what Herb Bonham told his daughter, that if Bonham Salt terminated their usage of slave labor, the planters and ranchers would buy their salt for their stock from Saltville, the largest Virginia salt supplier. This was a big problem for Rebecca: whether to relinquish the steady customers her father cultivated all these years. However, now she wasn't alone; she had a partner named Everson Golly who had a "new market" in-mind that he and the boys were now free to pursue if the new boss approved.

The Road to Saltville

Early in the new year of 1848, a few days after Herb Bonham was laid to rest in the church cemetery, Rebecca drafted and sent a hand-written notification to every Bonham Salt customer, some of them the wealthiest of businessmen in western Virginia. Most of these men attended their salt supplier's funeral service and knew that Rebecca would be taking over her father's business. They were all dismayed by her written words to them:

Dear Bonham Salt Customer: Since the passing of my father I can no longer continue using the slave labor my father contracted with you. This is a personal matter for me, and I certainly hope you will continue doing business with Bonham Salt. If not, I will understand. Respectfully, Rebecca Bonham.

The heir to Bonham Salt took her father's advice and got out of the salt block business to planters and merchants, since only *"slave labor made it profitable and gave it any chance of being a going concern."*

Table salt with iodine is what Ever wanted to market to Richmond households and restaurants. Ever told Rebecca about a doctor from Wales who made a fortune in Ireland in the early 1800s by putting iodine in every box of salt he prescribed for his patients. Everson's father was one of the doctor's iodine-deficient patients.

***

During those first weeks of cleaning up and tying off the remains of their dead salt block business, Ever and the boys were kept on the same salary by Rebecca, since she was more than obliged to keep her father's word and make her fiancé a partner in Bonham Salt. First, Ever and the boys had to take the bigger Bonham wagon pulled by the two brute male mules Jasper and Perry on an arduous 80-mile, 4-day trip to Saltville and back, hoping to secure a good price for the direct-to-consumer product Rebecca was financing in order to see if Ever's crystalized table salt would fly. Since Saltville was the only producer of this new method of salt brine paste into granulated salt –this was an important trip for Bonham Salt's future.

While little Dolly was staying in the Bonham house, learning to read and write, as well as rudimentary elocution and singing lessons with her peers, who were the children of wealthy land barons around Big Lick - the males of Golly Springs were on another important voyage. But first they had to stop at the Ajax Box Company in Big Lick, some 7 miles south of the Bonham house. The "Golly Springs" box was a critical part of this venture, and it had to be secured. This was the only credible company of its kind in southwest Virginia that manufactured these oblong-shaped cardboard boxes for products sold in stores, such as soap, sugar and coffee, cornmeal, rice and table salt. Rebecca had sent a letter in advance of this meeting to the general manager, a friend of Mr. Bonham's who would welcome the trio into his office. Also, Rebecca designed the cylinder-like box they wanted to use, similar to a large oatmeal container that they tested to hold 5 pounds of table salt.

Big Lick was one endless stream of dirty mule teams delivering wagonloads of products going north and south. By the time they'd parked outside Ajax Box Company, they'd

92

counted 32 wagons loaded with porcelain contained crystalized salt cakes headed north to the big cities beyond Virginia.

Having turned 20 recently, Ever, like most young men in 1848, thought their lives half over. *"Twenty is middle-age when you die at forty,"* Ever's father had said more than once to his son. So every day was precious to Everson Golly; and Ever made sure he passed on this appreciation for life to the boys by teaching them to stay open, to *"look, listen and learn when you encounter every living thing."* So much was this "present awareness" instilled in James and Buck that they constantly competed for praise from their surrogate father/big brother who was not much more than a decade older than the boys. And there was uncertainty about the age of James, for when Buck celebrated his 9th birthday in late October, Rebecca discovered that James did not know his age or the day of his birth. So resourceful Rebecca made a double birthday celebration out of October 29th, *"the day Buck and James turned nine years old,"* she proclaimed when she made two separate chocolate birthday cakes with 9 candles burning atop each one.

In Big Lick, the boys followed Ever into the old brick 3-story Ajax Building, each boy intensely interested in every aspect of their business. If James asked Rebecca or Ever a question –Buck was right there to hear the answer and recall as well as James could. Rebecca suggested they name their product on the box, *"Bonham Salt 5,"* which she explained, *"represents all five members of our family as well as the five pounds of iodized salt in each box."* When the family voted on what to call their product, "Bonham Salt 5" or James's suggestion, *"Golly Springs";* Dolly voted with her teacher's choice while Ever and Buck voted with James. Now Ever carried the exact size of box they wanted, as well as the baby-blue sample Rebecca gave him for their background color, plus the printed lettering: *"5 lbs. of table salt with iodine."*

Seated in the Ajax waiting area, it was Buck who had a remarkable idea that he wanted to tell Ever before his meeting with the Ajax boss.

"Ever, if we get a box that's good, we should have our customers give it back to us when their first box is empty. We can re-fill it and save on boxes."

James looked at Ever to see what Ever thought of Buck's idea. Ever was impressed, seeing right off that it would increase profits quite a bit per sale. "Great idea, Bucklin. Keep it to yourself until we get out of here."

That's all James needed to hear, that Buck could make a business decision; to James, that was incredibly empowering for Buck and himself, for now James began to think of the business as if he too could be a part of this risky venture in a new world. James and Buck were ready to use all their energies to help make their venture a success; all three of them believed they had been spared by God an early death in order to live life to the fullest extent possible in 1848 Virginia.

Ever called this business plan *"On to Richmond";* first they had to get the right quality container at the right price in order to market their product in the growing Richmond market. Pennies in 1848 were like dollars today; every penny counted back then, and Ever and Rebecca were good at watching their pennies. Rebecca had gone over the numbers several times and told Ever they could spend no more than 3 cents per box, since the cost of the iodized table salt had to also be no more than 3 cents for 5 pounds, because they planned on selling their 5-lb. box of Golly Springs Salt for 25 cents a box direct to households and restaurants without any middle man. *"Cash and Carry,"* Ever proclaimed to Rebecca, *"And no credit."*

It was amazing to Ever that he was able to get his baby-blue and white 5-lb. cylinder box for 2.5 cents per box with free delivery for a 500-box minimum order. Since the top of the box had to be sealed once filled with 5 pounds of salt –the Ajax owner threw in a gallon of glue paste at no charge for his new customer. Since Ever had to secure his salt price in Saltville before he could order the boxes, he hoped to stop at Ajax on the return trip to pay for his first order.

Off to Saltville they rolled with Ever holding the slack reins as Jasper and Perry continued their plodding walk south through the Big Gap. The boys pored over a history book given to them from Rebecca, a black and white pictorial with crude drawings depicting the location of American towns and cities with their teacher's handwritten notes about each location and its historical significance and dates. Her assignment was to memorize information she would test them on upon returning home. Both boys were motivated to learn by a sibling rivalry Ever appreciated. For twelve hours they rolled in 39-degree weather south on Great Road until it was time to sleep. They were about half-way to Saltville when they camped under a tarp on the wagon bed, warm and cozy thanks to the blankets and food Rebecca supplied for their trip. Dried beef with green beans and canned peaches was their big meal before hitting the hay, literally, for the trio had covered the bed with hay for a bit more comfort.

Earlier, the boys wanted Ever to sleep while they took turns at the reins; however, Ever knew there would be nothing close to a good sleep on this old bumpy road. Now, all they had to do was get a good price for 2500 pounds of iodized salt that they would hopefully haul back in 10 barrels, enough salt to fill all of

95

their boxes of product. Before sunset that first day, a few miles south of Big Lick, Ever realized he forgot to bring a salt block for the animals. Not much later, the boys witnessed how their leader can remedy a problem. It started with a whisper to the boys: *"Be grateful and good things happen."* The trio giggled about it under the tarp their first night in the Bonham Salt wagon:

Ever had spotted a resting team of haggard horses across the road and facing them; they were sharing a block of salt while the snoring driver slept on the buckboard with his back to the animals. Ever drove Jasper and Perry slowly across the road and up to the salt block, whereupon Jasper and Perry got their salt licks in, even breaking off a chunk of the block with their teeth to get the much needed salt. After this quick salt break –off they went. The boys, seated to the right of their driver, smiled at their good fortune to have such a clever man in charge, a man who now didn't have to remind his helpers to read their grammar lessons to each other.

Near sunset the next day they arrived in Saltville, parked their wagon across the road from a tavern at a water trough. They could use any of the salt blocks strewn randomly about and stacked in dozens of places in this busy and dirty little salt town of southwestern Virginia. Jasper and Perry especially liked the salt here, because the blocks were frangible and easy to bite off chunks, giving their feed *"added flavor,"* Ever joked. Dusk had brought cold weather fast. After placing blocks in front and behind the rear wheels the boys followed Ever toward the busy tavern to get a hot meal. They could see down the distant valley the vast sea of whiteness piled in the Lower Salt Works in what was called by locals *"Salt Valley."* They would go there tomorrow first thing.

The tavern promised warmth from a hearth fire that shot blue smoke from a blackened brick chimney. They could hear the raucous voices and laughter coming from working men drinking after a day's work in the vast salt wells and mines. Ever was familiar with such places; he'd been to many pubs in Dublin frequented by his father. He thought the boys should experience such a place where the men Ever likened to a circus show. They stepped inside the smoky din of these flush-faced men employed by the salt works here. The place was warm and ripe from the body heat of a hundred sweat-stained men of all ages. There was hardly a space to stand let alone navigate to the bar through a maze of strangers. The boys stayed on Ever's heels, inching their way along air streams of foul breath made of beef stew, beer and whiskey, all emanating from these men too drunk to care. One scraggly, angular man had a black eye patch covering one eye. He was following James to the bar and carrying his mug of beer.

By the time the trio from Golly Springs reached the crowded bar area Ever was having second thoughts about coming to this *"dark hell on earth."* Ever turned back to the boys and saw that the one-eyed man was about to pour his beer onto the head of James. Quick and sober Ever acted like a tomcat after a mouse, pulling James away in time; then: his powerful right hand gripped around the man's scrawny neck, raising him off the ground helplessly and literally squeezing the life out of his one good eye as he kept his grip and lowered the man to the floor. Ever leaned his Irish face close to the man's bulging good eye with his grip still on the man's throat he whispered, "Why would a man with only one good eye look for trouble?" Then he released his grip and ushered the boys outside quickly, knowing too well that alcohol and trouble were certain to hurt his mission.

Luckily, neither Buck nor James had seen what the one-eyed man was about to do. But now: they were hungry and cold as they headed back to the wagon. Ever had money for a hotel room; except he was a frugal man and liked to save money when he could. So again they huddled in candlelight under the tarp covering the wagon bed where they dined in relative warmth and comfort, savoring the variety of provisions Rebecca had provided in her large picnic basket.

They went to bed on the wagon's bed, huddled together in this cozy darkness with good blankets of goose-down, feeling content after their good meal as wind roared in the cracked openings in the canvas along with the sound of Jasper and Perry getting in their salt licks before sleep. Tomorrow was their biggest day of the trip, and they all knew it. They prayed for gratitude in all things before going to sleep. Then restful sleep came.

Big Mistake / Small World

"What are the chances," Ever whispered to the boys after taking their seats in the customer waiting area. He appeared to be some kind of foreman, not an office worker. Then: *"Patch Man"* noticed the red-headed man who gave him the bruise marks around his throat. Time for Ever to think fast, for now he feared his salt purchase was in jeopardy. He told the boys to *"wait by the wagon,"* not wanting James to experience any ugly scene.

Patch Man could only manage furtive glances at Ever while all Ever could do was pray that this man did not send them home with an empty wagon. The money Rebecca gave him for their salt purchase was now burning in his pocket, for he could see the man talking to other men about him and what happened in the tavern. The other men kept looking over at him and making comments to each other like other men will do when not alone. But then: Ever's mind was helping him, giving him creative ways he could turn this thing around in his favor, because *"after all,"* he reasoned to himself, *"this man would have hurt James in a most insidious way."* That's when Ever's imagination and his innate sense of justice made Ever stand and walk toward Patch man and his pals. The men were confused and wary as Ever got closer to them and then stood with them. Ever looked at the one-eyed man and asked him if he worked here. He nodded yes. Ever pointed his index finger at the skinny man and told him:

"You might have caused the loss of more business than you're worth to this company."

Ever could see the man's eye widening in fear again as it had last night after he told the man, "Tell Mr. Winslow that Bonham Salt is here."

It worked. All the men scattered, none wanting to be in the office when Herb Bonham's old friend, T. D. Winslow, came out to greet the fiancé of Herb's daughter.

Ever went back to his seat; but then it dawned on him that nobody had informed Mr. Winslow that he was here. Rebecca had informed Mr. Winslow at her father's funeral that her fiancé, Everson Golly, would be handling her future salt purchases. Winslow had expressed in his ever-present neck twitching, an earnest desire to accommodate Ever *"whenever he calls."* That was the leverage Ever chose to use on those men. He had seen his share of swine like that one-eyed foreman, and knew what they feared and respected: confidence.

Come to find out, the salt boss was not even on his property yet; he was due *"anytime he pleases,"* Winslow's secretary chuckled to Ever.

Outside, the boys were watering and feeding the animals the shelled corn and oats Ever brought from the Bonham livery. The boys knew the mules had to have a good meal for the heavy load going home.

"Mr. Winslow isn't even here," Ever said to the boys, hiking up his pants and wishing he'd worn those suspenders Rebecca gave him from her father's wardrobe.

All around them were salt-dusted teams pulling wagons in and out of the bustling Saltville Salt Company. James had his eyes on a wagon loaded with slaves that was headed for their daily work in the vast salt marsh, salt wells and mines that supplied salt to millions of people in all directions. Ever was well aware that salt was a valuable meat preservative as well as a necessary mineral for humans; and he marveled at how little it cost in relation to its importance for maintaining and preserving all life on earth.

Today was the coldest of mornings so far since leaving Golly Springs. Even though the cold north winds blew in freezing air, the buffeting hills around Saltville deflected most of it and made sunshine something appreciated. If not for running into Patch Man, Ever would've scouted around this operation, seeing how the salt was iodized and seeing first-hand where the barrels of salt were filled. From Rebecca's bookkeeping records she knew that the last barrel of iodized salt her father bought weighed 250 pounds and cost $7.50 a barrel or 3 cents a pound. *"Plus a dollar deposit on every barrel,"* the new owner of Bonham Salt told her fiancé in the quiet office that was not doing any business until Ever and the boys would begin their *"On to Richmond"* campaign selling salt to Richmond housewives and restaurant owners.

After an hour or so, Mr. Winslow arrived on horseback with a wagonload of slaves following him. It was obvious to Ever that James was looking at each man in the wagon as the *"Old Salt"* barked and twitched at the wagon driver where he wanted the slaves to work in his vast salt works. Buck thought the rich old goat with his bald head and bushy gray sideburns was funny to watch when he twitched his right eye and right side of his face violently when he barked his orders to his minions who watched in horror at his facial spasms , and no way wanting him to repeat a word. That's why the Patch Man and his crew high-tailed it out of the office: their boss was a taskmaster not to be tested or agitated one iota. Buck and Ever were aware that James was looking for his father in that wagonload of men rolling toward the largest salt marsh. Ever had asked James if he knew what happened to his parents. James had said he believed they were alive somewhere, adding, "*I never saw them killed on the ship, and I didn't want to look. So I look at everyone.*"

Ever had the boys wait by the wagon when he went over to Mr. Winslow to introduce himself near the office entrance, now recalling having seen the flabby-cheeked man at Mr. Bonham's funeral.

He was in Mr. Winslow's office for over an hour, listening to stories about Herb Bonham mostly, and what a good man and friend he had been for so many years. And Ever realized early on into his visit that Golly Springs --their new product secured at 3 cents a pound --was supporting slave labor as Mr. Bonham had for so many years. The slave labor that this operation was using was thirty times that of Bonham Salt. So, Ever bit his tongue, swallowed his morality standards and paid $75.00 for 2500 pounds of the best iodized granulated table salt available. As with Bonham Salt, Mr. Winslow waived the dollar per barrel deposit and trusted behind that liquid southern drawl laughter that of course "*you'll return the barrels back here to be re-filled when needed.*"

The old man and his new customer stood outside the office, so the boss could point out his loading dock, where Ever would pick up his ten barrels. But Ever had to ask the boss who that guy was with the eye patch.

"That's Snot," the old man drawled with a twitch.

"Snot? That's his name?" Ever laughed.

"Snotgrass. Everyone calls the boy, Snot," the old man chuckled.

"How'd he lose an eye?"

"That's a good one for you. That Snot got his eye poked out by a slave working here. Don't know why the slave did it, but the slave ran off and has not been seen since. Well, show Snot your receipt and give my kindest regards to Ms. Rebecca."

"I will indeed. Thank you, sir."

At the Bonham wagon the boys had cleared the bed of the wagon, making room for the ten barrels of salt to be loaded at the warehouse. Ever drove them over to the busy warehouse loading dock, where they saw Snot standing with his hands akimbo as Ever handed him his receipt. The foreman pointed to a stack of salt blocks and muttered for Ever to "Block your wheels." Four slaves came out of the dark warehouse and placed an iron ramp from the ground to the wagon's bed. Ever and the boys watched the men roll their oak barrels out from the warehouse, down a wooden ramp and up the iron ramp into the Bonham wagon. James was watching every move the men made. Before Ever drove his wagon away the foreman handed Ever a receipt to sign as one of the slaves removed the salt blocks from the Bonham wheels. Before Ever signed he looked down at the Patch Man and said to him in a calm voice, "Big mistake/small world." The skinny foreman averted his eyes without uttering a word. Ever handed back the paper and drove his mules away from the dock, their plodding walk slow and steady. Upon leaving the salt works and on the road headed north James asked Ever if any of the slaves were paid for their work. Ever explained how they got a roof over their heads and food. James had to know why the white indentured slaves had a contract and the black slaves didn't.

"I don't know why things are like that. Poor folk will always do the work for the rich," Ever said with resignation.

"I never want to work for anybody who doesn't pay me," Buck was certain.

"That's why you have to keep learning every day," Ever was certain.

James reached down for his grammar lesson under the buckboard and began reading out loud to his brother. It was clear to Ever that James was questioning the bondage of his people more than he ever had, and that was good, Ever knew.

They rolled north along this beautiful stretch of southwestern Virginia, a fulsome valley enveloped by hills and trees still covered by the silver frost of morning. As the boys recited their lessons, Ever could see that "slavery" was the big mistake his new world was making. And yet: Golly Springs was a part of it all, as Bonham Salt and every business was that managed to profit from it. *"It'll be abolished as it had been back home,"* he was certain.

Fabulous Fifties

The 1850s started out good and kept getting better for the Golly family. Rebecca and Ever have been married for 4 years and not able to have children of their own. Still they wanted a much larger house on Golly Springs even after adding on two large bedrooms. What a garden Rebecca tended on this fertile ground, yielding huge tomatoes and potatoes that were much bigger than the garden she had at her father's house, which Rebecca converted to a one-room schoolhouse that Dolly attended Monday through Friday. Ever and his wife worked out a schedule where Buck attended school one week while James worked the salt route in Richmond all week with Ever, returning home Friday evening. The next week James would go to school with Dolly and his teacher. This way the boys were getting educated and one of them was home all week to help take care of their home.

Buck objected more than James when it was Buck's time to go to school all week with his sister, for Buck loved working their route that began in Petersburg and went all over the hills of Richmond. Golly Springs had become a respected household name and staple product with their new delft-blue box with white lettering that matched the color of Dolly's eyes.

Rebecca held onto her father's land; and, she made sure that the 800 acres that made up Golly Springs, including the access road, was legally owned by Everson Golly. Two things had worked well for the ready-made family: Rebecca was left a rather large sum of money from her father's estate; and, Golly Springs salt deliveries to households and restaurants started out good and kept getting better. That first week, before the school rotation, Ever and the boys hauled 100 boxes of sealed Golly Springs Salt to sell. By early Friday they had sold every box for 30 cents a box cash and carry. Since the product was delivered to the customer's door, it was a fair price considering store shortages now and then.

Ever knew that the key to their success would be in three months when they stopped back to get repeat orders and the empty box. Thanks to their attitude about gratitude –all things worked better than imagined. Their wagon was painted the same blue and white colors of their product and Rebecca was working on sewing a blue and white shirt to be worn in the spring that matched their company colors. Their salt wagon was covered by a tarp to prevent rain and snow from ruining product, and 2 mules could handle the diminishing load for the week. The boys would fill the boxes from two barrels while on the way and seal them with glue. They would leave home Sunday evening in order to arrive in the Richmond area by morning. One of the boys would be sleeping while Ever and the other boy would take turns at the reins. Hours before dawn Ever would wake a helper to take the reins so he could rest before arriving in the sales territory they had mapped out earlier.

In summertime when both boys worked, Ever would knock on doors holding a full box of Golly Springs: "Good Morning, ma'am, I've started home delivery of my family's iodized salt. It's a five-pounder and if you save the empty box for when I return to re-fill your order I can keep the costs down." Ever would always sell more salt than the boys. James had the hardest time because of his skin color. He started out going with

Ever house-to-house holding a full box of the attractive blue and white container. By the time the boy with the big white teeth memorized exactly what Ever said to every prospect –he would let the rejection bother him –until Ever had Buck gladly skip school for a week and team up with his brother. It was a move Ever was glad he made because shy James got to see his fast-talking brother get sales at a pretty good clip, which indeed fueled the healthy competition between brothers that Ever felt James needed in order to break through his mind's barriers of self-doubt and rejection.

Since Richmond was by far the largest and wealthiest of cities in Virginia, Ever's goal was to have enough repeat customers until eventually every minute of the day of every business week he was only re-filling orders for them.

They began in Petersburg working their way house-by-house and to every restaurant and tavern. They worked their way north with Ever getting most of the sales. Buck started slow, getting a bit better every week he went out. Watching Buck sell was what inspired James to come out of his shell of quiet speaking with zero aggression –until Buck started selling more and more.

"It's just something you have to do by yourself," Buck tried to explain to his dejected brother. When Buck offered to practice with him, James waved him no, saying in his perfect enunciated English, *"No, I have to do it with the customers. I just know I must do this myself...like you said...and with more gratitude."*

That was the weekend Rebecca suggested to Ever that James skip a week or two of school to go out with Buck and see how they sell as a team on the route. Ever loved the idea. And it worked like a charm, if only because James could stand beside Buck while Buck pitched the *"lady of the house."* Bucklin Dunn was a little actor with a desire to please Ever by getting sales and earning the salary both boys continued getting every week. Ever was literally selling both barrels every week with consistent numbers that was giving him more and more confidence on and off his route.

In those early days of Golly Springs & Company, it was early spring and summer and frugal Ever had them staying in the wagon with the animals in the downtown Richmond Livery. The livery was where James got his first sale, to an old slave named Ozzie, who traded a box of salt per month if they could sleep in their wagon inside the livery and clean up at the water tank.

Upon returning home before dawn Saturday, the three of them would jump into the healing waters with their dirty clothes on, removing and washing them in the boiling water. Rebecca wouldn't tolerate any bugs brought back to the house. The water never failed to relax and rejuvenate them, returning light to tired eyes that seemed to dim by mid-week in the tiresome hills of Richmond.

Then came the fun part for Buck: Ever would hand him the leather shoulder pouch that belonged to Mr. Bonham; then he and James would lie on the floor or sit at the table and count the money from sales for the week, around thirty dollars, a tidy sum of money that Rebecca would deposit in the Virginia Commonwealth bank in Big Lick Monday afternoon when school was finished for the day. Usually one of the boys would drive her and Dolly in the carriage pulled by one of the horses now stabled with their animals in the barn they'd built that first spring on Golly Springs when Rebecca and Ever were newlyweds. Rebecca liked using her father's house as a school for some of the children in the area interested in learning basic reading, writing, and arithmetic. If the weather turned harsh she would spend a day or so living in the comfort of her father's house, a place she alone had made into a home.

Dolly was reading faster and writing with more proficiency than her brothers. The spunky little redhead with braided pigtails and two missing front teeth was anything but self-conscious about her lisp whenever reading out loud in class or reciting memorized multiplication tables that none of the other students could do as fast as Dolly Golly. Last Christmastime Rebecca had gone to the county registrar in Big Lick to have Dolly's and James's last name legally changed to Golly. Buck wanted to keep his name, Dunn, since he believed he would find his father one day in America. James wanted Virginia for his middle name. No matter what, this mixed collection of mutts was one family united in heart and mind no matter who was born a Golly or not.

***

So many fabulous things were going on in the 1850s for the Golly family. Rebecca had taught her husband how to clean, prime, load and fire the musket her father gave his future son-in-law. Ever became a fair hunter, bringing home two deer and a wild turkey one week in November from the west woods near their cozy home. Deer and other game were known to frequent the sparkling James Stream that rippled along the west woods and across the South Gap Road and bridge Ever and the boys reinforced over the years.

By 1853 Buck and James were in their early teens. Mr. and Mrs. Golly were making more than a home for their four children; they were giving them self-confidence, trust and security, consistent love and attention, as well as instilling faith in a loving God that was far removed from the sin and punishment dogma taught by so many Puritan-like people in

America. The ever-growing cancer of slave owners keeping millions of people in bondage for profit was a growing hypocritical subject in the Golly home and discussed openly. It was no accident that Golly Springs and Company never again sold their product to known slave owners on farms, plantations and business concerns. Many of the domestic slaves working in the finer homes of Richmond became Golly Springs customers if only because their men and mostly women were treated well enough to be considered *"part of the family"* –in most cases. And: more than a few of their 2,000-plus repeat customers on their Richmond salt route were dropped when a slave was seen or heard being treated badly. One such indent took place when Ever and James were working a well-to-do Richmond residential neighborhood:

James had heard a young woman's screams of agony coming from the back of the large Victorian, a good customer of theirs. When James went to the back of the house to see what the commotion was about, he was shocked to see a white woman whipping a young servant's bare back while two other slaves held the poor woman down. James hurried to find Ever and told him what he saw. All Ever could do was to tell James that they would never deliver salt to that house again. And they didn't…until James Virginia Golly was 15 and curious about that young slave girl who was whipped badly, a girl he discovered who had his middle name.

Sweet Virginia and Face Look

T he Golly Springs salt route couldn't have been going more smoothly when James stopped his wagon in front of the white 3-story Victorian, that same house where he'd seen the young slave girl getting whipped over three years ago. Meanwhile, Ever was downtown on foot going door-to-door into businesses carrying his order pad as well as one box of product to show to new prospects. Boss Ever loved writing up repeat big orders to his restaurant/tavern customers that he and James would deliver later in the day and the next morning. To all their customers, they were a grateful duo.

James was caught up on his residential route of happy customers who ordered multiple boxes at a time. He was due to meet Ever for lunch at one of their better downtown customers, The Commonwealth, a fine dining establishment that bought 20 boxes of salt every week. These days, Golly Springs and Company delivered six barrels of salt a week, bringing home most of the ninety-six dollars a week, a considerable amount for one family in the 1850s. James had been selling as much as Buck by shear persistence, coming back time and again to households who never bought –until his big toothy smile finally got a sale; then off he'd go to the next house, most often to deliver a box or more to a regular. Then he'd grab a sample box and try to sell a new prospect. James Virginia Golly loved his work, and most of all he loved the freedom he enjoyed compared to others of his race in 1850s America. Most were domestic slaves; or, some could be indentured servants who also lived on the premises, according to the contract.

James was getting a reputation as a young educated free black man who dressed and talked like an educated white man. Most of the James Golly customers in the Richmond area respected him, since he kept coming back to deliver and get back the empty boxes *"to keep our salt price down,"* was the logic the trio used at every delivery and sale they ever made. And it worked like a charm.

Now, with a bit of leisure time before heading off to meet Ever, and as his mule licked its salt block while parked on this narrow residential street of brick cobblestone –James carried a box of salt to the front door of the house where he'd seen the slave girl whipped years back. This was *"Pemberton House";* neighbors and regulars on his route would tell James that the slave girl he inquired about is *"Virginia."* He'd been planning what he would say to the old Widow Pemberton with the constant scowl when she answered her thick mahogany door upon using her lion head door knocker. But Virginia, attired in domestic apron, answered his knock, smiling at *"The Salt Boy"* she'd seen many times over the years.

"May I help you?" she drawled in such a frightened tone behind her smile that he thought he actually scared her.

"I'm sorry to disturb you. I'm James Virginia Golly and I must admit that I know your name to be Virginia," he smiled that winning grin of his that intimidated her a bit as he held his product in front of him with both hands. To her, this was the mysterious *Salt Man* that stopped delivering to Pemberton House, but all the other homes he'd stop and deliver his salt. Yes, Richmond domestics liked the free delivery, since meat had to be preserved with larger quantities –nobody missed toting salt for miles across Richmond up and down the City of Seven Hills.

She nervously rubbed her hands over her gray apron, the color of all domestic uniforms in the huge Pemberton House. James watched her every move, even her quick straightening of the red head scarf tied over her short nappy hair that was not visible –another part of the *"Pemberton Code of Standards"* the widow would post for all to read; yet none of her domestics could read or write much, except for Virginia, who was always bothered by the fact she could read and write but very little.

"Is Mrs. Pemberton in? I'd like to see if she would like to get back on my salt route?" James asked with a bold confidence she liked, along with the way his diction was so perfect.

"So you own this business?" she pointed at the blue box he was holding."

"Yes, my family owns it," he smiled proudly with a joy on his face she didn't see often around here.

"I thought that man with the red hair owns Golly Salt?" she drawled sweetly.

"He does. There's five of us in our family."

"But he's a white man?"

"All of my family is white," he laughed. "It's an interesting story I hope to tell you some day."

"Mrs. Pemberton isn't feeling well enough to receive any visitors. Come back next time when she feels better," Virginia drawled.

"I will," James bowed his head respectfully when leaving , then added with a smile, "See you next time."

All day long James thought about the girl named Virginia, and how beautiful she was up close. During lunch with Ever downtown beside the James River, he talked to Ever about the slave girl he saw today, *"the one I saw getting whipped behind the Pemberton House when we first started the route."* Ever recalled the incident and how that was why they stopped calling on the austere widow.

"How old is she?" Ever was curious.

"Don't know…and don't care," they laughed together.

"What did she say?"

"It's not what she said, Everson"; James smiled, "it's her genuine sweetness that impressed me. And to think of her getting whipped now that I've met her…it angers me. I am most anxious to see her again."

"Call on her next time 'round," Ever tried to cheer up James.

***

Next time turned out to be two weeks later when Buck and James started riding together in one wagon because school was out for the summer; that's why Ever drove alone in a smaller Bonham Salt wagon converted to a Golly Springs wagon. This way Ever could haul 2 of the 6 barrels with one of Mr. Bonham's big mules while another team of mules led the way pulling the boys and 4 barrels.

The boys loved their new independence where Ever worked one street and they worked another. Now they were free to talk

114

about girls and other people and things that came their way along their route without Ever's conservative business-like attitude when on the route. At 16, Buck had quite a sense of humor that was far different from James or Ever. Buck could see funny things in awful circumstances or laugh openly upon seeing people who looked funny to him. Buck was at his funniest when he would quip to his brother, *"Face Look,"* and that meant James was to look at the face of the nearest person, whereupon Buck would burst into laughter, causing James to laugh. Most of them were old man with some funny feature that Buck would point out to James, and this would go on all day long. The confidence gained from selling and meeting so many people over the years has given Bucklin Dunn this bold assertiveness in every situation that James often envied and tried to emulate when he spoke to Virginia.

It was during this first week working the route together without Ever that brother Buck made one of his bold moves that forced James to call on the Pemberton House again. Buck, at the reins, turned them onto the street where Pemberton House was.

"Where are you going?" James was more than alarmed.

Buck didn't say a word until he stopped in front of the Victorian mansion where Virginia worked and lived. Then, Buck turned to his brother sitting beside him on the wagon and told his brother matter-of-factly, "You know how some white folks won't buy from you?"

James nodded yes, and listened.

"Well, I think the old Widow Pemberton is one of those. She never would buy from you. If you go up there now and you don't sell her, then you come back and try again later…she could tell you to not come back. If that happens…you don't see this

Ms. Virginia again. But if I go up there and sell the old widow 'cause I'm white, and when she gets to liking our service again, like we know she will, that's when you start delivering. Does that sound like a plan, James Virginia Golly? Or would you rather try and take your chances?"

James looked away from his canny brother; then, he looked at the imposing Pemberton House on the hill with the imposing lion's head doorknocker that he could see from the parked wagon.

"Go ahead," James said quietly.

Buck reached back and grabbed a box of product and exploded off the wagon like a cat going after a rat. He watched the back of his brother's red head moving closer to the Pemberton front door. James hoped that the sourpuss widow answered her door instead of Virginia, who would surely see him from the front door and wonder why he wasn't calling on her "master." The thought of "*master*" caused James to clench his jaw and tighten his throat as if some ineffable wrong he felt in his heart and mind was causing his body to tense and feel his white-hot anger from the image of that sweet Virginia getting whipped by that mean old woman.

From his vantage point he could see Buck purposely blocking anyone's view of the Golly wagon from the front door of the house. The flabby-cheeked widow answered her door and scowled at the young Irish kid holding the blue and white salt box over his heart.

"Good day, Mrs. Pemberton. My name is Bucklin Dunn and my family owns Golly Springs Salt. And this here box holds the best iodized salt in Virginia. This majestic home is the only house on the block that doesn't use our product. For thirty

116

pennies, this here five-pound box of Golly Springs Salt gets delivered to your door when you need it replaced. Will you please give us a try again?" he smiled and extended the box to her.

"Wait here," she ordered the freckle-faced young man.

In a few minutes Buck came back to the wagon without the box and with a big grin on his face when handing James the receipt copy of their new customer.

"You sold her," James smiled big.

"You bet I did. But next time you can deliver and maybe see your sweet Virginia."

"Did you see her?"

"No. I saw the Widow Pemberton herself, a *face look* if I've ever seen one," he laughed when taking the reins. "I did good not to bust out laughing when she counted out her thirty pennies like it was the last ones she had. The rich ones are the tightest."

Far From Innocent / Sin and Punishment

Virginia Langdon, along with her six siblings, was the first generation of her family to be born in America. Most of her family lived near Wilmington, North Carolina; she'd been sold to the Pemberton's for four hundred dollars seven years ago when she was 10 years old. Mr. Pemberton was alive then, finding the girl Virginia when on a business trip to Wilmington. She was sold on the Cape Fear waterfront auction block in Wilmington the same time two of her older brothers were sold to North Carolina planters. Mr. Pemberton's aging wife needed a domestic because her health was declining.

On that sad day in Wilmington, young Virginia had watched her shackled brothers led away to a wagon and roll away on the brick streets of Wilmington, never seeing them again. *"And I never will,"* she would tell other domestics working in the Pemberton House, doing her best to accept that she may never see any members of her family again. She may have looked helpless that day getting whipped by Mrs. Pemberton's hickory switch with the velvet tip - that never left scarring and rarely drew blood - yet Virginia Langdon, Widow Pemberton's sweet domestic was known to be one tough survivor by any standards; and yet - she was known to be self-conscious about the fact she didn't know how to read and write well enough to suit her

118

nagging desire to be educated. This was a source of shame she wanted to conquer. *"But how?"* she'd ask herself every day. The answer always came back to her with the same true and ugly answer: *"Mrs. P. wants you dumb. There's no school for me here. And Mrs. P. shore won't buy no books for me to read."*

"Ginny," was able to let go of the past more than most folks. That's what other domestics said about her. *"That Virginia may look and sound sweet, but that girl is far from innocent."* That's what Mrs. P. was thinking each time she whipped the 15, 16, then 17-year-old domestic for sneaking out of her room at night to walk around Richmond. At every whipping the same words repeated by Mrs. P. that Virginia carried with her far longer than the sting from the hickory switch, two words that only left her mind scarred: *"sin"* and *"punishment."*

***

Selling and competing with Buck during the summer months made the time pass swiftly in sweltering Richmond, where each oppressive summer month was even more humid than the month before. Washington Avenue was coming around again for James on their salt route. Not wanting to lose the new Pemberton account because of the widow's aversion to James –again Buck called on the big house; once again he rapped the lion's head on the solid front door. He heard footsteps approaching and placed the delft-blue box with white lettering against his heart, a superstitious sales ritual that Ever practiced and passed on to the boys.

Usually the second box was easier to sell to a customer. It was also easy for Buck to see why his brother liked the slave girl named Virginia from the moment she opened the front door. And those quick emerald-blue eyes of Bucklin Dunn saw clearly that she had to be *"sweet Virginia,"* because of the way her dark

119

butterscotch-colored eyes shone disappointment that it was not James holding this second box of salt she'd been waiting for.

"Ms. Virginia?"

"Yes," again surprised that another man from Golly Springs Salt knew her name.

Quick-thinking Buck was ready, just as he and James had practiced for this moment if Virginia answered the door. But Virginia was also ready and told Buck to wait, *"I has your money right quick, sir."*

Upon returning, handing Buck the empty box and 30 cents in coins, Buck handed her the new box and told Virginia discreetly that there was a message inside the box *"from my brother James."* He felt sort of bad when he walked away leaving her feeling confused about the message.

Inside the Pemberton pantry she could open this *"message from James."* She opened the box and found a folded piece of yellowed parchment that Rebecca had given James –along with his teacher's advice, *"to keep the note short, sweet, and to print the letters so they are easy to read."*

She couldn't open the note now, for two reasons: to be caught with such a thing from an admirer meant certain punishment lashed out by the old widow who did not want *"my girls doing anything untoward or sinful with any man"*; and –she really couldn't read much at all, for she was an expert at faking her way through, pretending that she could read and write better than most uneducated young women.

The shame of her illiteracy overcame her when she fisted the note and hurried to her cubbyhole room off the kitchen, closing the door to the only room of her own she's ever known, a barren

5'x 10' storage room that now held her cot and bedside dresser drawer she'd found outside one of the homes on Washington Avenue and was allowed to drag home. She wanted to open the note from James now, and she did, staring down at the printed words that formed no words for her. The strain from trying to make sense of those letters angered her to tears of frustration. Nobody at Pemberton House could she trust to even tell about the note, for fear they'd tell Mrs. P., since the slaves working here were always looking for ways to please the "master." The thought of that word made her so angry that she realized she'd been squeezing the note in her hand so tight that she was crumpling and creasing something that was more valuable than anything else she owned right now.

***

All day long James thought about Virginia and the note he hoped she could read. By the end of the day when the Golly men met at the downtown Richmond Hotel, where they ate in the hotel's restaurant and stayed four nights of every week instead of in the livery with their wagon. It was Ever who bartered to supply all the salt for the hotel's restaurant in exchange for one evening meal and lodging Monday through Thursday nights. Since the hotel's massive kitchen used about 10 pounds of salt a day to preserve the meat they stocked, a reserved room with 2 beds was reserved plus a meal for the Golly men as requested in even trade. *"For a little salt we all sleep in a warm bed,"* Ever told Rebecca of the deal he struck with the hotel's owner.

***

Summer's heat diminished considerably by September; and so much so that one night Virginia had slipped away from the Pemberton House when she was certain that all were asleep. She'd had the unread note from James for too long fortnights and would not wait any longer to find out what his words were. From experience she knew that the salt wagon was due to stop soon and she wanted to be able to respond to those mystery words printed in bold letters that reminded her that she too was like her kin, unable to read or write anything at all.

It was the time of night in Richmond when not a soul was on the streets. Her plan was to find a white person as close as possible to the Pemberton House who could read her note from James. She had to be careful, for Richmond was getting a bad reputation as a city where northern men of despicable character would find black women and children they could take, then sell them to businessmen and planters on the busy slave blocks all along the southern coast.

"I has to be careful," Virginia kept telling her fearful mind along these quiet dark streets of Richmond that always thrilled her intensely. *"A black woman who can't read or write has to fear strangers more than anybody,"* she reasoned, holding the note clenched in her fist that was made by the only free black man she knew and admired. *"He has a good job and comes from a good family,"* she'd tell her discerning mind many times since meeting James Virginia Golly. *"Maybe James can teach me to read and write just enough to understand the little things that I has to pretend to know every day,"* she'd tell her yearning mind.

Further and further she walked until thoughts of turning back dominated her instinctive caution; now she was desperate and willing to approach the first white man she saw in order to accomplish her goal. Not a soul was in sight, telling her mind that *"nobody is up this late but tired folks too tired to sleep."* Then: up ahead on the next block she knew there would be mostly women at work at night in the Peabody Garment Company. Some of the women were older black women who

122

worked for a dollar a week as indentured servants in the clothing factory.

From the dark street she could see the lambent yellow-orange candle-lit interiors of all three floors of *"the sweat shop."* She figured she could just go right in there and show the note to the first white person. The thought of working here vanished when she recalled how comfortable she really was in the Pemberton House. She had good food and a roof over her head, compared to this noisy and drab monotonous maelstrom of weaving, fabric dying, sewing and a thousand patchwork tasks going on all at once at hundreds of little stations on three crowded floors that were deplorable working conditions.

Virginia moved cautiously considering all the noise going on around her in a thousand places. She passed an open door in a dark hallway, whereupon she saw a white man with black and white whiskers mumbling out loud while writing down figures with the aid of two candles burning on each side of his paperwork. Long hesitations were caused by her fear until she thought of how she must be getting home soon. Standing in the man's doorway she cleared her throat to get his attention. He appeared surprised to see anyone standing in his doorway.

"What is it?" the man was obviously annoyed.

"Please excuse me, sir. I was hoping you could read me this here note," she unclenched her hand and revealed to him the note.

The man waved her over to him and extended his hand to read the note under one of his burning candles. He read it out loud without emotion:

123

"Sweet Virginia, how dare I think of you so often and wish we could spend time together. Respectfully, James Virginia Golly."

She repeated the words to herself when he handed back the note.

"Thank you, sir, I am most grateful," she bowed and exited the building in a hurry.

All the way back home she repeated the words to herself, until under her bedcovers safe and warm and then the same question: *"How will I ever spend time with him?"*

Law of the Land

A round the middle of the 1850s, California was luring men to the depths of gold fever. Richmond was buzzing with the news about California becoming the 31st state, upsetting the balance between 15 pro-slavery to 15 anti-slavery states. Ever was explaining to Rebecca at the dinner table one Sunday how northern politicians had to give something to the southern politicians for off-setting this balance of power: *"So now they made it a law of the land that runaway slaves found up north by bounty hunters can be captured and taken back to the slave's owner. They seem to be going backwards,"* Ever complained to his wife. Then Ever told his wife of the increasing angry talk that he hears in Richmond all week, that, *"slavery was the law of the land in the South, and that damn Yankees* should mind their own business."

Dolly would repeat something learned in the classroom, then adding her own take on things that amazed her teacher, all designed to provoke James into speaking out after she'd said, *"Washington and Jefferson owned slaves. Rich people from every country have made slaves of people to keep labor costs down. And most of the slaves I've met seem perfectly content where they are."*

"That's because they don't know freedom. I know freedom," James would say with such confidence that both he and his sister were surprised.

125

Ever would voice his concern about how a great war could be fought over slavery.

"Since we live in Virginia we have to fight with the south, *right?"* Buck asked Ever.

That's when Rebecca intervened and said, *"Nobody in this family is going to fight for any side in any war, and that's the law of this land."*

Ever and the boys had no choice but to nod in agreement. That's when Ever and Rebecca agreed to save back a barrel of salt from their 20-barrel delivery every three weeks from Saltville to stockpile their inventory in case things heated up regarding state secession. Rebecca, more than her husband, wanted her family to be *"prepared for anything."*

Anything

Over the next two years the ambitious Golly Family continued improving their home by adding on three rooms and a fireplace for the master bedroom. They enlarged the main room and kitchen along with adding on a front porch that skirted half the house on two sides that faced south and east. A row of pointed firs were planted by Rebecca and Dolly on both sides of the South Gap Road in order to one day give the approach to Golly Springs a stately appearance that would in time afford any visitor a narrow then widening view of their ever-expanding home.

James was allowed to spend more time with Virginia at Pemberton House ever since the widow has been confined to her upstairs bedroom with severe arthritis that crippled her body and made her even more impatient with her staff. Unable to watch over her domestics, the widow was on the warpath, constantly harping and accusing Virginia and others of stealing and sneaking out at night to be with men.

By 1858 it was obvious to Ever and the boys that the *"anything"* Rebecca wanted to be prepared for –was secession and war. From house-to-house in the finer neighborhoods where the rich and influential lived in the capitol city, secession was the forgone conclusion for the increasing *"Yankee meddling"* in the South's way of life. It was 18-year-old James Golly who believed that the South would never go to war to protect slavery.

127

Despite all the vitriolic words shouted at or around James when on his salt route, he and the other Golly men were trained by experience to keep their opinions to themselves, to sell and deliver their salt with a smile –no matter what slurs and rigid beliefs were hurled in their direction.

Yes, silence is golden in business; however, in matters of the heart –that is another matter altogether. For two long years James has been bringing and picking up primary readers to Virginia with every salt delivery. These were the same beginner reading books Dolly learned from. Now, Dolly Golly at 13 is being tutored to attend an all-girls school in Derwent this fall, the same prestigious school Rebecca attended for three years before returning home to help her father run his business.

***

Early September of 1858 it rained all morning the day Ever drove Dolly and his wife in the Bonham carriage to enroll Dolly at the all-girls school in Derwent. James and Buck followed them in both wagons loaded with product and would break away for a week on the salt route some six miles from Richmond. Ever would escort the girls to Derwent while Rebecca helped Dolly get enrolled and situated in her new living quarters on the quaint campus not far from Richmond. Mr. and Mrs. Golly would stay in the Richmond Hotel, a room adjoining the reserved room where the boys would stay after their day on the salt route. On Tuesday, Ever and Rebecca would pick up Dolly at the private campus and take her shopping in Richmond. Dolly really liked her roommate Gwen, a planter's daughter from Charlottesville. Gwen was two years older than the girl with the *"unforgettable name,"* Dolly Golly.

Parasols, fashionable dresses, laced leather dress shoes, along with exotic perfumes were things Dolly bought, wanting to fit in with Virginia's privileged class of females that were destined to bear the first generation of children to live in a new sovereign country that would break from The Union. Dolly and Buck were alike in that they wanted to know historical facts about prominent figures and how much things cost to convey an image of prosperity and a bright future. James understood his siblings too well, confessing to Rebecca that *"Dolly and Buck were ashamed of being poor early on, while I didn't know I was poor until I looked back on it from a safe place at Golly Springs."* James Golly was all about feeling; he dismissed facts as something uninteresting to him, *"too much trouble to save in my precious head,"* he'd laugh while pointing to his nappy head. He would notice things nobody else in the family thought of: like how Rebecca's pronounced Irish-American Southern accent was taking over the Golly way of speaking, *"because she is our teacher and we imitate her."* Only Ever kept his Irish sound, as if he had stepped on Virginia soil for the first time yesterday.

Ever understood Dolly and Buck's desire to never again be so poor and helpless that they could be held in hell watching their mother die in a stench-filled darkness. Ever knew what Dolly and Buck's mother wanted for her children –a better life. That memory of watching their mother vanish into the sea was on Ever's mind that day of shopping with Dolly in Richmond. He found himself praising his daughter more when she was so happy to be buying things for her new life at school: *"Dolly, you are a lass of good taste that will serve you well. I so want good things for you, Dolly."*

"I know," she smiled at the man who was more of a father figure to her than he was to the boys; she saw Ever more as a protective older brother who had saved them from a world that was more brutal than kind.

Amidst all the red-faced wizened whispers of secession in the prosperous Richmond business district, Ever now saw his beloved wife as this light of grace and care that loved their life together, making a fine home and future for children she did not bear. And not only the children of Golly Springs, for during this decade of being the husband of Mrs. Golly he had seen how hundreds of children from the area were openly grateful for the education they received from her alone. Almost every holiday at Bonham House and Golly Springs former students would visit their teacher and bring her little gifts of appreciation to show their gratitude for the world of learning she alone revealed to them over hundreds and thousands of days filled with lessons and recitations, all made under the patient and tempered pace of a saint in the throes of her mission: *"To teach children to read and write as well as they possibly can."*

Today, that *"anything"* Rebecca and Ever had been preparing for, saving a barrel a salt every week, was today the smartest business move they made. Nearly 200 barrels of iodized salt were stored in the old Bonham barn for the trouble that was coming to Virginia. Walking the sidewalks of downtown Richmond they heard the arrogant, saccharine pride of Southern aristocracy and specious entitlement in their genteel bowing while greeting and departing on these busy streets of Richmond:

"Good mornin' Ms. Pettegrew; I do wish you the very best on your recent endeavor; And please give my fondest regards to Mr. Pettegrew."

James, more than anyone else in his family, could see this vainest denial, this collective masking of the stench and cruelty of slavery going on in every other household in Richmond. Richmond was indeed a rebel city preparing for something bigger than anyone could comprehend: Rebecca's *"anything."*

Stolen Night

By early 1859 it was apparent to the Golly Springs men that Richmond was getting closer to having one calamitous event that would lead to secession and war.

"It's inevitable!" Mrs. Dundee declared to James in that liquid southern drawl, a sound of supreme self-assuredness that James grew to detest. However, his next call was across the street at Pemberton House where surely his *"sweet Virginia"* would be waiting to see him.

She had heard the familiar clip-clopping of the salt wagon approaching. This was the day she has been thinking about for over two years, the day they would spend time together doing other things besides learning to read and write with departing secret kisses and warm embraces that only made living here harder to take. Mrs. P. was bedridden 24/7 and even more cantankerous, threatening to have Virginia sent to South Carolina to a planter she'd heard had an evil reputation for raping and lashing his female slaves. Just days ago her bedridden owner had made herself clear by shaking her palsied and crooked finger at Virginia, warning her, *"If you ever try to leave my charge you will have hell to pay by me! Five hundred dollars is the price your boyfriend can pay for your flesh! Don't ever forget that! And don't think for one minute I don't know what you two black rabbits are up to!"*

Those spiteful words spoken by an evil woman bounced around in Virginia's head as she waited outside on the front steps for James to deliver his box of salt. The fisted coins, moist and warm in her sweaty palm reminded her that five hundred dollars was too much money to ever come by in a lifetime let alone soon enough to ever hope to have a life with James Virginia Golly. This was a man she could love, because he was free; he alone could rescue her from the bony curved fingers of that witch upstairs. She dropped the coins into the empty box like she'd been doing of late.

Sweet Virginia had a plan and it was time to tell James part of it. She rehearsed the words in her mind like she memorized the alphabet and words in the books he had given her. The words she'd written on the same brown parchment used to cover fish from the market. James had given her a lead pencil that she kept sharp with a straight razor "borrowed" from the kitchen since stealing was the biggest of sins and got the most lashes. It was easier to visualize her plan when she saw it printed out in her own hand and memorized for three fortnights. Once her brain knew every word –she burned the words in one of the three Pemberton fireplaces.

Then: she could see James approaching from the street with his blue and white box of Golly Salt; he was so handsome to her, wearing that black bowler hat with black suspenders he and Buck bought together three months ago from a peddler on Petersburg Road. She would laugh more than once a day ever since James told her that his brother would wear the hat and suspenders one week and he would wear them the next week. After a while the hat would slide down and nearly cover his eyes since Buck's head was bigger than his brother's. She could see him standing at the Pemberton front door with his hat tipped way back on his head and his explanation of it. And she'd laugh out

132

loud when alone, knowing this is what it feels like to love someone you want to always be with. Now, as he neared in his tipped hat and suspenders holding up those maroon-dyed trousers Rebecca made him –she led him over to the alcove hidden by a pair of pointed firs where they kissed and held each other after he placed his delivery beside the empty box that held thirty cents.

"I has to tell you, James…"

"Have," he corrected her behind his impish smirk, then kissed her forehead below the gray head scarf Mrs. P. made all her girls wear, a symbolic color loyal to the new Confederacy. Virginia hated what it represented and finally said:

"I have to tell you, James, I'm leaving this house tonight and going north where I have a chance to get my freedom, like you…have."

"Now just how are you going to do that when they chase down slaves up north? They're called bounty hunters, Virginia. You do know about them? They will find you and bring you right back here. Then you're really in trouble."

His round face was so earnest and true.

"I don't care no more. I can't stay here no more with that mean old woman, changing her bed, empty her toilet while knowing I can read and write. And she says I can have my freedom for five hundred dollars."

She watched his brown eyes thinking over the next words he was about to tell her:

"When is the house asleep?" he whispered while moving his gaze to the west corner of Washington.

133

"About ten," she whispered, her eyes dancing with his as he thought things over.

"Meet me at that corner tonight just after ten," he nodded to the west corner. "Bring what you can carry. I can't bring a wagon. Too many would see us," he seemed to be repeating his thoughts as she nodded in agreement with him and leaning her head to his chest she cried his name into his chest.

His strong hands enveloped her thin shoulders and whispered to her in that earnest tone she loved:

"I can't let you go north. You can stay at Golly Springs with my family."

"Are you sure?" she looked up into his eyes.

He nodded yes and she kissed him. Then, he went back to pick up both boxes of salt, handing the new box to her. On his walk back to the wagon he was numb from her price for freedom since five hundred dollars was too much money to ask his family for; and, it would take too long to save that much money. He was glad tomorrow was Friday, their last day of the week on the route. He continued on, his mind busy with future things he'd be doing as the wagon habitually stopped at the next customer's house. Instead of now going over their quick time together on the Pemberton porch, his mind was racing, planning every detail: like what he would say to Ever when he left the room tonight; and the long drive back home with Virginia riding beside him with Rebecca preparing their big meal for when they arrived safely at Golly Springs. Then, the bad thoughts came, just as they would whenever he saw a man, woman or child of his color mistreated or suffering in any way. Many times Virginia had told him how the Widow P. questioned her about her "*nigger salt boy,*" and threatened her by warning her if she ever ran off with him *"I'll know where to find you, and both of you will pay dearly."* Those were the exact words her master said, and more than once. *"Ever will know what to do,"* James tried to calm his mind and hopped down from the wagon after getting two more boxes of salt for the last two customers on this block of Washington Street.

***

This was the last night in January of 1859. It was cold enough that not many would be out and about at 10 P.M. when James would meet his Virginia on the corner of Washington and Broad Avenue. He decided to walk, since his wagon was a familiar sight and sound for nearly every household in Richmond. Walking fast with yet a few blocks to go he was certain Buck and Ever hadn't heard him leave their room, since they usually were asleep fast around nine. He hadn't told them of his plan because he decided that it was best not to involve them –in case they would be seen or caught.

Many times James had heard of the great lengths white slave owners had gone to retrieve their *"property."* It seemed like the heightened fever pitch of secession all over the South had also increased the resolve of slave holders to go any distance and meet any cost to track down runaway slaves wanting to break away from this new country soon to be called the Confederate States of America.

He thought he was early upon reaching the place of their meeting; however, she was already there, shivering and waiting with her meager belongings bundled inside a burgundy-colored blanket that when draped over her shoulder reached the back of her calves. She put the blanket on the frozen earth when he arrived and kept her arms folded in front of her chest when he embraced her. He could see that the old tattered coat she wore

135

wasn't nearly warm enough for a night below freezing. Gentleman James removed his best dress coat, a full-length black trench coat lined with black rabbit fur that Rebecca gifted him from her father's wardrobe. Her thin body shivered in the warmth of the fur that his body heat generated during his walk to reach her.

He picked up her bundle and they started walking back the way he came, toward downtown Richmond, his long coat reaching to her ankles and her bundle slung over his broad shoulder.

"We's stealing this night, ain't we, James Golly?" she laughed knowing he never talked that way.

"We's shore is, Ms. Virginia," he drawled and they both laughed loud and long.

"Oh, James, let's keep laughing as long as we can," she seemed to be pleading to him.

More laughter came as they walked briskly on the vacant brick road that was slick from wear and cold.

"Where do we go now?" she asked her rescuer, both snorting cold air with every breath.

"I got us a warm place for the night," he said.

It bothered his heart to know that he was the only black person allowed to stay in the hotel, because Ever and Buck were white and they supplied the salt for the hotel's restaurant. And yet: he never had to actually tell her she was not allowed to sleep inside the hotel –she already knew.

"We'll spend the night in the livery. I have a bed prepared for you in the wagon. Ozzie sleeps there with the animals. I told him I'm bringing my girl for the night and he don't mind."

"Doesn't," she corrected him and they both laughed.

"Is Ozzie a white man?" she was curious.

"No, he's like us."

"Is he a slave?"

"No. He lives there for his room and board."

"Then he shore isn't like me. He's free."

"I suppose that's right. But you're free right now."

The 2-mile walk to the livery had tired James more than Virginia, since normally he'd have two hours of sleep by now inside his warm hotel room. Toothless and gray Ozzie answered the knock on the livery door with a lantern raised to his stocking-covered bald head to discern who this was with the Golly Salt customer.

"Ozzie, this is my friend, Virginia."

The old man winked at the young and pretty girl before stepping back and allowing them to enter the warmer space of the clean livery that smelled of sweet hay and straw mixed with the pungent aroma of horse and mule flesh.

It was considerably warmer in the livery as they followed Ozzie's lamp and bowed legs over to the three stalls where the Golly wagons and animals stayed. James placed her bundle on his wagon bed while Ozzie thoughtfully left his lantern and mumbled walking away, "It'll help keep the chill off a mite."

"Thank you, Ozzie," his guests said in unison as they watched him saunter off into darkness, walking on the outside edges of his feet, suffering with a painful case of rickets.

James got into the wagon bed and helped Virginia up after clearing some space for them and making a bed with the warm blankets he'd brought down from his room before going to meet Virginia. He folded one blanket to make a pillow for them to share as she curled up beside him on the wagon bed with the lantern warming them.

"You warm?" he whispered, facing each other on their sides.

She nodded that she was.

"Well, this shore 'nuf ain't no Richmond Hotel," he scooted closer to her and they laughed.

Staring into his lit brown eyes, she asked him, "What about tomorrow?"

"Now we sleep to get our rest to handle tomorrow."

She smiled in agreement and he cradled her head against his neck in the golden flickering lantern light, not wanting to tell her tomorrow that she wouldn't be able to have a big breakfast in the hotel dining room with his family. And now, from this moment on, "slavery" was James Virginia Golly's enemy to be revisited and fought until it was vanquished forever.

Free and Rich Young

Friday morning, Ever and Buck were a bit concerned that James was not in the room when they awakened in their hotel room, for they knew how much James enjoyed the big breakfast in the hotel dining room. After breakfast and upon arriving at the livery, when they saw that the wagon was gone - they figured James wanted to get a good start on his route. Ever thought since James was behind Buck in delivered sales for the week, that James might've skipped breakfast to catch up with his brother.

This was the day James was to work the route on Franklin Street, a long stretch of several blocks whereupon he'd work one side of the street all morning; then, he'd turn the wagon around and work the other side of Franklin all afternoon. When James was finished for the day, he'd be a short distance from crossing the James River, where soon afterwards he'd meet up with Ever and Buck at Petersburg Road for their return trip home together.

All Friday, after only a sub-standard breakfast of bread and boiled potatoes James bought from a peddler outside the livery and shared on the wagon with Virginia, James was most anxious to have his family meet *"sweet Virginia,"* this mystery girl owned by the Widow Pemberton and vicariously tutored by Rebecca's lesson planners.

The day on the salt route was especially anxious for Virginia, who kept thinking how her master would suspect that she had run off with the *"Golly Salt Man,"* and that any minute some bounty hunter would come to take her back for severe punishment. Several times throughout the day of busy deliveries James would tell her that she was now *"free"* and that he would not allow any bounty hunter to take her back.

"What about next time you deliver your salt to Pemberton House?"

"I got that all figured out. I'll ask for you when I deliver, and when they tell me you're not here I'll ask where you went."

"Mrs. P. will still believe I went with you. There's no forgivin' or no forgettin' with that old mean woman."

"I tell you, Virginia, you are free now, and the sooner you believe that the better off you'll be."

She knew he was right, although it was easy for him to say, since he was the only free black person she had ever known or seen for that matter.

Buck and Ever were happy to see James when he met up with them on Petersburg Road south of the city. Both Ever and Buck came over to the wagon to meet this Virginia that Ever hadn't met and yet heard so much about over the years. Each one took her hand in his when James introduced her from the buckboard of the wagon. Ever was a perfect gentleman, *"pleased to meet you,"* as well as affable Buck, who had delivered the message in the salt box that made this all possible today. James and Virginia followed the other two wagons headed west for home. Ever was most anxious to talk to James about his "mystery girl," hoping they didn't get married fast or elope before having time together. Since James was known by the family to save nearly every dollar he made, Ever thought it was possible that James negotiated her freedom by paying the

140

widow. Buck knew what his brother was doing, and promised his brother he would not say a word to Ever or Rebecca, *"Or Dolly,"* James made Buck promise.

Buck was in the throes of a bad case of gold fever, paying more and more attention to the California gold strikes along the Sacramento River he was hearing and reading about in Richmond. Since the beginning of the family business, Ever kept his word and split the profits three ways evenly between Ever, Buck and James, after the costs of salt and the expenses for the week. Each week was better than the last with wagons being loaded with more and more product. Bucklin Dunn wanted to be rich young, not just plodding along the streets of Richmond making a good living for 80 hours a week selling and delivering and driving to Richmond and back.

That's how James and Ever were alike: they could see the patient long haul paying off down the road at a steady increase in security for the family. Ever could see the confidence Buck was showing week after week by selling more and more product to customers, therefore giving Ever the time to call on new prospects. Ever knew that Buck was spending the little free time he had inside the Richmond Mercantile; he was getting prices for all the equipment needed to be a gold prospector. *"I can get all the supplies I need at half the cost that those vultures charge in California,"* he declared to Ever. Word was getting around that it was the merchants in California who sold supplies to the gold-thirsty prospectors who were striking it rich. Every now and then some lucky prospector would hit a vein, and word would spread to those young dreamers of fast wealth –and thousands more would head west.

Bucklin Dunn was one of those dreamers of fast wealth; and both Ever and Rebecca knew it was a matter of time before he left home.

"We should get him a good sound wagon for such a journey and a team of animals to get him there and back," Ever told his wife.

"Yes, we must. And a team of animals he can use on the route until he leaves, a team who will know Buck and serve him on such a long journey," Rebecca said.

"Buck has driven more miles to Richmond and back, enough miles to go to California and back ten times. I have the confidence in him that he can get there and back on his own," Ever smiled.

By the time the Golly Springs wagons reached South Gap Road late Friday evening, Virginia had heard all about the Golly family history from James. He explained to her that Buck wanted to go west to find his biological father as well as striking it rich, just as James wanted to find his parents that were stolen from him on the sea.

"So Buck thinks his father is in California?" she asked her driver.

"Yes, he thinks his father is out there looking for gold."

She could understand looking for parents stolen at sea, since she was taken away from her family and sold to the Pembertons.

"But why would he go so far to look for a father who had left his family on his own?"

"Because he knows that his father felt he had nothing to offer them…so he never returned. He bears no hard feelings against his father. Buck told me one time that the older he gets, the more he understands his father."

Virginia understood what James was saying, for she did not blame her parents for letting her be sold to the Pembertons.

Nearing home late that night, the Golly wagons rumbled over the small bridge crossing James Creek, "affording us a shortcut of many miles and less trouble," James said to his passenger, who felt safe in this hidden oasis named Golly Springs. The worn road was a smooth ride, for each wagon slipped into and rolled along in familiar ruts, tracks made by these very wagons over thousands of trips in every kind of weather. Leaving the south woods Virginia could now see the solid-looking Golly home with clouds of blue-silver smoke floating out of the chimney toward the full moon illuminating the house. James kept his eyes on Virginia's face, a beautiful face emanating pure awe and joy at the sight of this hidden oasis that was far removed from the daily bondage in Richmond. The animals pulled with increased vigor and knew the way from habit, turning left at a narrow fork in the road that led to the barn.

"Oh my, James, this is Golly Springs?" she asked sweetly, as if she'd died and gone to Heaven upon finally seeing this home James had told her about in their stolen moments together.

By the time they'd parked the wagons and put the animals in the barn, Rebecca came out in her winter coat and shawl with the usual lantern in hand. Virginia watched Ever and Rebecca kiss and embrace so lovingly, she thought. Rebecca waved at Buck and curiously she waved at James and his companion wearing his black coat; it was then that she realized this must be "sweet Virginia." Rebecca gave James the lantern while she hugged and welcomed the smiling Virginia. This kind of welcome from loving people was something she'd missed for so long, and tears of joy came.

143

The Golly men promptly cleaned up and sat at the ready table to enjoy the late meal of venison and potatoes and carrots with fresh rye bread after Rebecca said grace. Virginia sat next to James in Dolly's chair with Buck across from them and Rebecca and Ever flanking them at each end of the heavy oak dining table. All were making a point to let their guest feel welcome and comfortable in their home.

Virginia slept in Dolly's room; although a small bedroom –it was at least four times the size of her cubbyhole room in Pemberton House. Upon opening her balled bundle of belongings she found her red leather Bible and worn primary lesson books; there inside the Bible her collection of notes James had brought her in his Golly Springs salt box. These were her most valued possessions, words she'd pored over hundreds of times; and here she was - in the loving home of the Salt Man. Because of these people in this wonderful home she too could read and write and truly dream of freedom. Under Dolly's covers she thought of all the exciting things Rebecca told her. Tomorrow they would bake pies and cookies to be served after Sunday service. Then Monday her teacher said she could go with her to Bonham House to increase her reading and writing skills. It all seemed too good to be true for Virginia, to find this kind of family in Virginia where aristocracy ruled and slavery was the energy that sustained it. And then her busy mind went back to the exciting words spoken by Buck during a relaxed conversation before the fireplace with everyone listening to his plans to leave for California in the spring. She couldn't remember ever being in the midst of a family expressing their wants and desires in such a supportive and comfortable atmosphere. Rebecca, James, and even Ever waited on her as if she were white and free. Several times she caught herself imagining the door bursting open and white men with torches dragging her outside to be returned to Pemberton House.

"I'm free," she kept reminding herself. *"I'm free."*

Now, only in the silence of a sleeping house she could admit to herself that she wished she could go with Buck to California, as far west as possible, to a new world that Buck said was the country's last frontier. She had asked James if he would go to California in search of gold. His negative nod told her that he had no such dreams, and told her, *"I like it fine right here, thank you."*

And now: she thought of her momma and daddy in Wilmington and how long it had been since she'd seen them. It was still true today that she would never return to Wilmington to see her family. That's what she'd told James when she first started seeing him on his route. She could hardly believe her answer when James had asked her why: *"Because they didn't fight to keep me."*

Safe and warm under the covers in Dolly's comfortable feather bed, she realized that she had to fight to keep herself free, vowing right there that she would never return to Pemberton House no matter how long and hard the South fought to keep slavery alive.

Fort Golly

That early March of 1860 the Virginia Commonwealth burned with the fever of secession. This real possibility of war made Buck all the more determined and anxious to make his way to the California gold fields. He figured he couldn't be *"forced to fight in a war if I'm clean across the country."* Ever and Rebecca maintained their belief that the Golly Springs men should stay out of the war while supplying Richmond households and businesses their salt. However, rumors were flying that the new government would force all businesses to supply the army what it needed in order to defend the Confederacy from the north. Thousands of men and animals had to have salt. And the Confederate dollar was taking hold. Small family businesses like the Golly Springs family feared they'd end up with a depleted inventory and worthless paper in the bank.

"What can we do?" Ever asked his wife.

"We can only go with the flow of things…and hope for the best," was her answer.

***

By April the Golly family was preparing for Buck's adventure to California. They all chipped in and made sure Buck was clothed and supplied with the best equipment for gold prospecting. Buck was outfitted with a tent, blankets, lamps and fuel, winter clothing and boots, along with a supply of canned fruits and vegetables that Rebecca and Virginia put together. Rebecca even bought two young male mules from an estate auction along with enough feed and salt to keep the mules pulling the same wagon Buck used on his salt route. The wagon was a gift from Ever *"as long as you return with it,"* was the sincere stipulation for such a gift.

The last day on his route before leaving for California, Buck stopped at Dolly's school in Derwent to say goodbye to her. He hadn't seen Dolly since the Christmas holiday break and could hardly believe how his soon-to-be 16-year-old sister had matured. Dolly met her brother on the lawn of the school grounds in front of her dormitory. They strolled around the verdant campus talking about her plans to return home if war came, explaining in her educated flair:

"Most of the students here hope for war, ignorant of the deprivations war will bring to all Virginians. I cannot bear to be around them when death and destruction arrives. You and I have seen death at an early age, haven't we Buck?"

Buck's solemn nod was in agreement; then he wanted to give his explanation for leaving home:

"This will be the first time I have left a home that I know I can return to. That alone gives me the confidence to make this journey across the country. Ever made our lives safe and comfortable. I want to risk myself doing something I did all by myself...then return to Fort Golly as my own man."

"Like Ever did?" she asked.

"Yes, like Ever did."

"Rebecca has told me so much about Ms. Virginia in her letters that I feel I already know her. Do you think they will marry?" Dolly asked her brother.

"I think so." Buck half-cocked his head to one side and grinned for what he was about to say next: "Ever since Rebecca has been teaching her at the Bonham School, Virginia is able to express herself better. And James tells me she threatens to go off to some school up north to get herself educated and meet some smart negro like Frederick Douglass ."

"What does James say?" Dolly laughed.

"Oh, he pretty much ignores it. But I did notice that James is reading more these days now that Virginia is reading more and more books."

"That is exactly what happened when Ever and Rebecca got married. Ever was reading just to keep up with her," Dolly laughed. "So when are you heading off to California?"

"In a few days. I know there's always a wagon train of Mormons leaving from Saint Louis that I can ride with most of the way."

"It's safer in numbers, Buck," she advised her brother.

Then Buck removed an oval-shaped tin from his pocket that Rebecca had given him to hold and preserve the blurred image of their father, the only photo he had of the adventurous man who had come to America alone. He flipped open the tin and she took it from his hand, studying it thoughtfully before saying, "You think he ever came back for us?"

"No, I think he's still here. If there was ever a man who would join a gold rush –he would," Buck said with certainty.

"Perhaps you will find him in California," Dolly smiled at her brother's approaching adventure.

"I won't be looking for him much. I'll be looking for gold nuggets. And when I find them I'll come back and build us a bigger house on Golly Springs with a new barn and plenty of horses to fill it."

Dolly began to cry, knowing that her brother was just like their father –a dreamer. For a moment she lost her poise when she grabbed her brother's coat lapel and in a tone of anger, "Now you come back to us Bucklin Dunn, no matter what you find in California. And do not forget that for one minute." She pointed to the tin and told her brother, "Don't you be like him and never come back to us," she cried into his chest.

He put his arm around his sister, understanding how she felt, and consoling her by telling her that he'll always return to her and Golly Springs.

***

Buck rode alone on this last wagon ride back home before leaving for California. Petersburg Road was thick with suppliers and farmers and sinister-looking speculators on their way to Richmond. He could sense the panic coming to the South and how even the slaves seemed to promote this heightened sense of fear and uncertainty coming. There was also this calmness inside Buck that knew Fort Golly (which he so-named Golly Springs during this threat of war) would not be penetrated or forced to surrender by joining up with this growing fever of the Confederacy. Ever put it best when he told his family but days ago: "*How can we fight against the South when we live here? And yet, any of those fanatics would burn us out of our beds to fight for their cause. If we fight with the South we fight to*

149

preserve slavery." It was then at the dinner table Buck saw how Virginia and James looked at each other and knew that Ever was right about remaining neutral. *"And we must fight to protect our neutrality if need be,"* Ever continued. But then James made his point: *"I hear that a big army is going to need all the salt they can get, and pay us in Confederate dollars. And if the Yankees get a hold of Saltville we're out of business anyway."*

Whatever came to Richmond, Buck was confident that Golly Springs would be a neutral place until all things were settled. That was on Buck's mind during his night approach to James Stream Bridge, a spot where Rebecca wanted some kind of gated entrance indicating that people lived here. Upon crossing the bridge and when the house was in view he stopped the wagon on the dark lane to take a long look at the home he promised Dolly he'd return to. A mental reminder to always see Golly Springs as this distant safe harbor was already instilled in Buck as he continued on toward the glowing lamp on the barn door that Ever left for his late arrival. The path was automatic for his mules, as was the hunger to be satiated inside Fort Golly.

When War Comes

B y mid-summer there was not a word from Buck letting his family know he'd arrived in California. Resistance to war by big business in Richmond was being heard above the din of youth calling for a new, independent country to raise the Rebel flag and *"whip them Yankees."* Ever and James would bring home news every week to Rebecca and Virginia concerning the prospects of war. Twice since Virginia left Pemberton House, James called on his customer inquiring about Virginia. Each time, he was able to deliver and get paid by a domestic without any message from the cantankerous widow regarding Virginia's whereabouts. It did seem strange to James that there was no mention at all of Virginia running away and no threats sent his way from the bitter old woman.

That summer, James proposed to Virginia; the ex-slave/domestic was now Rebecca's best student and accepted his proposal on one condition: that she could one day be certified by Rebecca to teach English and basic writing skills to slaves and indentured servants.

"I want to be certified to teach folks how to read and write," she told James. "There are hundreds of folks in western Virginia that must learn these basic skills."

James was most eager to agree to her terms, and so they were married in the same church as Ever and Rebecca in August. It was Everson's idea to help James build a home for James and his new bride on the southwest corner of Golly Springs, where the land was cleared and level with easy access to fresh water. They sorely missed Buck's labor and figured they could do no better than to get the foundation and floor in before winter set in. And that's exactly what happened.

Christmas came and went with still no word from Buck. South Carolina voted to secede from the Union, *"and war was just a matter of time,"* Ever said.

By April, when the frame to the newlyweds' house was all but finished and the wood shingles were ready to be hammered into place —Virginia legislators voted to secede and soon Richmond was destined to become the capital of the Confederate States of America.

It was during this most incredible period, when the South was preparing for war and Richmond had swollen to three times its size to over one hundred thousand, that James found out from a domestic neighbor of Pemberton House that charges had been recently filed against James Golly by Mrs. Pemberton after the widow found out that a James Golly had married a negro girl named Virginia. James went right over to the front door of the widow's house, prepared to do battle for this woman who was now his wife and thus united and free *"like all people must be."*

Outside on the front porch and behind the heavy door he could hear the rumblings of approaching war on hard heels overhead on her bedroom oak floor. An upstairs window opened above his head, to the ranting of a mad woman:

"Salt Boy! Step back so I can see you!" she commanded with such enmity in her tone that James wasn't real sure he was safe within her view. When he stepped back into the sunlit lawn, holding his box of salt, he could see the flabby jowls of an old and wicked woman shaking her pale finger at him, ranting, "You cannot steal my property and get away with it!" she drawled with all the volume her Rebel yell could muster.

"She's my wife, Mrs. Pemberton!"

"Not until she's paid for is she anybody's but mine! I can have the marriage annulled and you jailed for theft! This bill of sale is my proof and you will pay dearly!"

"How much do you want for her?" he had to ask.

"Five hundred U. S. dollars in paper or gold!"

"I'll give you two hundred in U. S. dollars and free salt for as long as you live!"

He could see that his offer had caught her by surprise when she hesitated and then agreed to his offer.

"Here's the first payment of salt!" he raised the box. "I'll bring the money next time around!"

He left the box of salt on the Pemberton porch and headed back to his wagon knowing he had to have this agreement in writing before he paid the old woman for Virginia's freedom. He couldn't stop thinking about how he should've called the old woman's bluff and just left without a word. Except: he had heard many a horror story over the years about runaway slaves who were shot on sight or even hanged for stealing property from whites.

By the end of the day, James had reasoned that he had done well by making his offer and getting the slavery issue out of their lives once and for all. He would tell Ever of the lifetime free salt delivery for the widow, who James didn't think would live another year or two at the most. Rebecca was good at drawing up contracts for things and perhaps would be his witness when the two hundred dollars was paid and the transaction completed.

***

Before the next delivery to Pemberton House –Fort Sumner surrendered to the Confederates and the war officially began. With Richmond, the new capital of the Confederacy only 100 miles from Washington D. C. it was obvious that more battles would be fought on Virginia soil more than any other ground in the whole country.

The city of Richmond seemed to explode into this war frenzy overnight. The pace of the public had increased markedly to the Golly men. Now the faces and eyes of the anxious men and women were flush with war and a grim determination to stay out of the Union. It was this same palpable feeling of pride about his feelings for human chattel that forced James to keep his accepted offer from the widow to himself and to remove the widow entirely from the salt route. He had decided not to tell anyone about the offer, even his wife, because the war was on now and his Virginia was content helping Rebecca educate the children enrolled at the Bonham House School, a school that was now supported by church members who paid the expenses for running a school for their children in this rather isolated area north of Big Lick that was now getting busier by the day since war broke out.

***

The early battles, raids, and skirmishes took place in northern Virginia; Rebel victories were luring more and more southern men with their home-state regiments to Richmond,

154

where these green volunteers had to be organized, outfitted and drilled to the best degree an agrarian society could muster.

It didn't take long before Golly Springs customers – feeling the pinch of isolation and war – started paying for their salt in Confederate money. Shrewd in business matters like her father was, Rebecca Golly convinced her husband to stay on the salt route, but to spend all their Confederate dollars for construction supplies and furnishings that would turn Golly Springs into the safe haven they all wanted for every member of their family that would include future generations to come.

***

This increased spending to build Golly Springs went on for two long years before the frazzled new government was confiscating all materials that were needed to make war and supply the Confederate armies in the field. This reality eliminated the hopes of staying in business; the family voted unanimously to stop their salt route and stay out of the war. Bold and audacious Yankee cavalry raids were hurting the South's breadbasket in the Shenandoah Valley in northern Virginia by burning all crops in buildings containing them. Grant was put in charge of all Union armies and more carnage was evident from there on. A neutral family, although rare, had to be ever watchful for both sides. Since Golly Springs was not supporting Virginia in any way, desperate Rebels didn't need much of an excuse to torch it. *"And who knows what Yankees will do if they come here,"* Mrs. Golly voiced to her husband. *"They'll take our supply of salt, our stored grain, our animals, and loot our homes."*

***

Nearly three years of war and now out of business, it was Ever's idea to load the remaining barrels of salt and salt blocks they'd saved over the years in two wagons and drive them over to the Confederate hospital in downtown Richmond beside the James River, not far from Ozzie's livery. Rebecca agreed with her husband that the Rebel army and their animals needed the salt, *"and we can't just sit on it."* Not all of the Golly family agreed with Ever that they can't live in Virginia and not do anything for the men and animals that die every day on Virginia soil. *"We'll take it there and the rest later if it can help at all,"* he told his family. *"Hospital or not, this government wants to keep slavery alive,* James agreed with his wife, adding, *"And I have a problem helping anything that promotes it."* When Dolly visited Golly Springs she was asked to break the tie regarding the salt matter, however she refused to vote on any issue regarding *"this awful war,"* and kept the neutrality she had managed in school. She was more concerned about Buck and why he hadn't sent word of his whereabouts in over two years. *"He promised me he would return home,"* she broke down at the dinner table in the home of James and Virginia.

By the time Dolly's visit had ended, both James and Virginia had changed their minds about giving their salt supply to the Confederate hospital. Dolly wanted to ride along with Ever and James to the hospital, to see some of the brave men she had heard about at Derwent. Ever decided to let Dolly ride along, since he knew it would be easier on the animals to pull an empty wagon up the hills leading to the school. He also decided to take only one wagonload of salt, with Dolly riding between James and Ever. All along Petersburg Road they could see that war had come to Virginia. Walking wounded men hobbled along on both sides of the road; wagons carried wounded soldiers and many hauled the covered remains of kin to be buried at home.

On one stretch of the road they passed a single line of male slaves a mile long; each man shouldering a shovel and headed for a train in Petersburg that would take them north to bury the dead cavalry men and horses left on the battlefield north of Richmond.

The Longest Ride

Both Golly men wished Dolly hadn't come along by the time they rolled into the James River warehouse district in downtown Richmond. The city was busier than ever with soldiers coming and going, some haggard from hauling the dead and wounded to the hospital after a battle; others were exhausted from bringing captured Yankees to holding areas at Libby Prison before transporting or marching them to the vast prisoner of war camp at Andersonville. A wounded Rebel soldier who rode in the ambulance wagons from the battlefield would say they had been on the longest ride of their lives.

Ever knew right where to go; he had this uncanny ability to memorize streets and places and the quickest way to get there. From thousands of hours on every possible road to Richmond from Petersburg –Everson Golly knew just where to go.

Outside the hospital they could smell death on the empty wagons stained with blood, parked two wagons deep all along the front of the hospital that faced the river. Ever went inside the hospital entrance to find out where he could unload his salt while Dolly and James stayed on the wagon…until Dolly wanted to go inside to see what war had done to these brave men and boys who suffered and died for a way of life she'd resented because of slavery. She'd heard it in the sultry southern dialog of the privileged young women attending Derwent. James tried to stop her from going, for he didn't trust the desperate characters

158

around the wagon; these were tired men who were armed and white and numb from wholesale carnage.

"I'll be back shortly," Dolly called back to James, raising her gray Derwent hemline a bit to avoid getting her dress soiled, then picking up her pace to a prance until she reached the hospital's front entrance. The hospital corridors and every spare inch of space seemed to be filled by a wounded soldier. She saw Ever walking toward her when he called out her name in the noisy lobby where the wounded called out in pain as nurses worked to comfort them in these overcrowded, chaotic surroundings. Ever pulled Dolly away from the gaze of a dying young man who was begging her for help.

"We have to unload next door at Libby Prison," Ever informed Dolly, taking her by her arm and hurrying outside with her, away from such a sorry place for witnessing human pain and suffering.

James was also relieved to roll away from the hospital after giving a bunch of armed Rebels all the salt they could carry away. Once parked outside the stark and massive Libby Prison, they waited a good hour before the prison storekeeper came out to show them where to unload the barrels of salt.

During the unloading of the wagon Dolly became bored and curious about the prison that was known to hold many captured Yankee officers. She wandered away into a storage area far from the men unloading the wagon. A door led to a long, dank and musty corridor that was unlit and soon reeked of garbage and damp bricks covered with green mold. It was a damp kind of cold here, so close to the river, "*this perfect spot for a prison,*" she thought as the moving heels on her ankle boots moved and echoed from the hard red clay underfoot. "*Nothing here,*" she told herhelf and turned back before going further.

She was hungry and anxious to go to the Richmond Hotel's dining room, where Ever said he'd buy them lunch.

The thrill of being inside a hospital and prison had worn off by the time Dolly reached the Richmond sunlight, and just when the men had finished off-loading the last barrel. Soon she could tell her roommates she had been to these places and had even seen these brave, dying soldiers fighting for a cause, a way of life that made rich men richer by allowing slavery.

***

They parked outside the Richmond Hotel and were enjoying their lunch when a black-mustachioed middle-aged man in a wrinkled black suit stepped right up to the Golly table, removed his hat, bowed liked a gentleman toward Dolly and stated with a cool southern drawl, "You sir," pointing to James, "are under arrest." When James stood up to protest, the lawman displayed his badge and holstered weapon by spreading open his coat. Ever made James sit down and asked the man what this was all about.

"Mrs. Pemberton of Richmond has filed a judgment against this negro named James Golly for stealing her property."

"How much is the judgment?" Ever asked.

"Five hundred dollars," the man produced a paper that he showed Ever, which in turn James read; then Dolly looked it over.

"It'll take me until tomorrow to pay this judgment," Ever told the man.

"You can pick him up at the Richmond jail across from the telegraph office after you come in to honor this judgment, sir."

160

Dolly and Ever watched the man follow James out of the restaurant.

"He's a private detective," Dolly said.

"He's a bounty hunter," Ever elaborated.

Ever didn't find out until later that it was the Richmond Hotel manager who tipped off the bounty hunter that James was dining in the hotel. For this the manager would receive half of the bounty hunter's share, as promised.

The ride to school was the longest ride for Ever and Dolly, each of them aware that James was alone again, riding a vast sea of uncertainty in a white man's world of *"property."*

"Men of property rule America," Dolly railed on their ride to Derwent, a beautiful ride except for the circumstances.

"And women of property," Ever made his point regarding the Widow Pemberton.

Dolly wanted to ride over to the widow's house to offer her the two hundred and lifetime salt as James had recently told Ever he had made with the old woman and accepted it. Ever explained that James called her bluff, not wanting to buy her back like she was a piece of property; and that Virginia agreed with him, not wanting to pay the woman a dime for her freedom.

"I fear those bounty hunters. I've heard they sell black people to other buyers and they're never heard from again."

"You fear that happening to Virginia?" Dolly asked Ever.

"And James," Ever said.

161

After Tomorrow

It was in the early evening when Ever rode alone back to Golly Springs after dropping Dolly off at school; that's when a Confederate captain was dispatched by Jefferson Davis to secure slaves and march them seventy miles north to Fredericksburg. The dead had to be buried from the Wilderness Campaign. It would be a burial detail made up of hundreds of wagons converted to ambulances. The wounded needed to be transferred to hospitals in the area along with thousands of Rebel dead needing burial in two different cemeteries in Fredericksburg.

Captain Bordon took one look at the well-groomed James Golly in the holding area and told the bounty hunter to *"release that man at once."* When the bounty hunter explained that the *"Golly negro"* was being held for property theft and that he would be released tomorrow when Mrs. Pemberton was paid their court-ordered judgment, the captain paid no attention to the paper produced to prove his case.

"Release that man at once. He will report back to you when he's finished. The judgment will have to wait. The country needs him now."

*** *

James was the best-dressed black man of the entire burial detail, a collection of men that included hundreds of slaves and free black men who were ordered to *"retrieve and bury our southern sons and brothers in arms."*

After every major battle, small-town citizens from all over the country would come to find their dead relatives. It was all such cruel work, to look and try to find the dead or wounded or missing. Gruesome work was ahead for this all-negro burial detail, let alone the hassles created by these people looking for missing loved ones.

Dolly and Virginia were anxious for Ever to deliver the $500.00 to the private detective hired by Mrs. Pemberton so James could return home. The women wanted to ride back to Richmond with Ever; however, they finally agreed that it was not prudent for them to go into a city mad with war.

The next morning, Ever hit the road again for Richmond with the money he needed for James's release and Virginia's freedom. Now Ever was seeing hundreds of stragglers, Rebels who had seen war up close and lived to tell about it. The things they saw were awful things they preferred to never talk about – for the rest of their lives. Most of these men were the only witnesses of deaths that had to be told to people back home they knew well. That's why the roads to Richmond were busier than usual. Wagonloads of hopeful families would now and them recognize a half-dead walking soldier from their town and inquire openly about their loved one, trying to find out any information.

The Wilderness was the battle that Ever kept hearing about, this place near Fredericksburg that sent these tired men home for good. Ever had seen these kind of men before on the gray wet streets of Dublin long before he came to America. They were the same kind of men he'd seen as a boy when the famine hit hard. It was a different kind of war back then, nonetheless –the faces wore the same look of pain and suffering. These were all men who had been deprived of a good life when young and now had to live after witnessing war to a degree that brought them here, on tattered shoes that had splashed through mud and blood and brains to reach this point on earth. Ever could see these men had been to hell and back; and soon Ever was about to find out that James Golly was on his way to The Wilderness, leading hundreds of slaves on a burial detail that Marsh Robert ordered via President Davis.

***

Riding shotgun on the lead ambulance wagon, James had no doubt that any one of these handful of Confederate cavalry assigned to accompany the burial detail would shoot him in the back if he tried to escape. Proof of this happened only a few miles outside of Richmond when one of the young black men marching at the rear of the detail high-tailed it into the nearest woods, whereupon a Rebel on horseback vanished in pursuit until…all heard the sound of a pistol.

The old ex-slave at the reins of the wagon James rode in, said he was "*a free man after my master died and gave us all our freedom. He wrote out his signature after tellin' everyone we free. Most of us don't know what to do,*" the old man confessed to James. "*Some wanted to be bought again jus' to be taken care of. Not me. I'm free,*" he cried out proudly.

"You get paid for this work?" James asked the man.

"No. Jus' food and water."

"How is that free?" James pressed.

The man made his point when he asked James how much he was "*gettin' paid for this work.*"

***

It was Ever's gut feeling to follow the road that went to Fredericksburg before turning northwest to the horrific battle near Spotsylvania Courthouse. A straggler told Ever he'd seen the long ambulance train of wagons *some ten to twelve hours back.* He went on to say, *"I's seen my share of that work after Antietam. That's what they'll hate the worst: buryin' dead horses and mules for Granny Lee!"*

"Why do you call him Granny Lee?" Ever was curious when sharing his canteen with the man.

"Oh 'cause he's so fussy about everything."

***

A few miles south of Fredericksburg, James and his massive burial detail stopped to rest for the night. James and his driver curled up on the wagon bed with their backs to each other. Before long, James told the man his name and inquired of his.

"Sam Webb. Soon to be free and livin' up north...away from these white devils that kill each other for nothin'. You'll see plenty of the white man's killin' ways tomorrow, James Golly."

"What do you mean by soon to be living up north?" James was curious.

"Grant's comin' south and he shore won't quit till every Rebel or Yankee's dead. After a big battle like this here Wilderness...things quiet down and the roads are clear for a few days...all the way to Maryland. Otherwise we be buryin' white men and their animals till we're just as dead as they is. There's no end to it. After tomorrow, James Golly...after tomorrow."

165

Bucklin Dunn

B ucklin Dunn was not a loner. He'd learned from Ever the gift of sizing things up, seeing smart ways to making money without slinging a pick axe looking for the mother lode, a vein of gold that was about as easy to find as a needle in a thousand haystacks. After three weeks of going from camp to camp in Sacramento, meeting and conversing with dozens of grizzled prospectors, he found out that after *women, whiskey and tobacco,* a good canteen made of aluminum that was light and had a well-attached strap was at the top of the list. Buck found the best canteen around from a Mexican named Pablo Garcia, a Sacramento businessman who agreed to sell his canteens wholesale to Buck for one dollar per canteen. Buck, after years of prospecting for customers, knew he could sell a quality canteen to thousands of men at five dollars a canteen.

Another ingenious business move that Buck made: by naming his canteen *Bucklin Dunn,* he'd be getting his name out there for his father to hear if he was out here in California. Buck had been planning such a business plan over the long wagon ride to get here. His salesmanship was proving to himself every day that he could survive without his family. From the first stranger he met to the most recent in Sacramento –he made everyone aware of his name and his new product.

The Bucklin Dunn Canteen would be his golden ticket to prosperity, pitching every gold-thirsty man flocking to California. Buck was aware of "false claims" of big gold strikes that were intended to keep a steady flow of men pouring in from all over the world. Every prospector would recall the bold blue and yellow printed letters *"Bucklin Dunn"* painted on each side of his wagon bed, a gift in Rebecca's artistic hand the day before he left Golly Springs for California.

It was easy for Buck, for he had used Ever as his motivation to persevere and prosper before contacting his family. That's why he had to have something to sell to these men and right away. The young entrepreneur left Golly Springs with $800.00, enough money to sustain him until a *Bucklin Dunn Canteen* was a quality product known by every sweaty, grubbing prospector who could read his name on the side of his wagon and see the five or six canteens hanging from the side by its leather strap.

"Best canteen in California is five bucks! Right here! Come get one!" he'd bark out to every man within earshot of his wagon.

Nearly every thirsty prospector or a drifter with five bucks and in need of a good canteen, bought from this traveling salesman named Bucklin Dunn. This red-headed Irish young man was more than surviving –he was prospering. Buck's goal was to make it big so he could have his family come out to California until the war was over. The real fear of Ever being dragged off by Jeff Davis to fill Granny Lee's trenches was driving Buck to selling 20 hours a day, every day. After 9 months of incredible sales he had banked enough money to think seriously about going back for his family. However, he couldn't go back until sales slowed down. They never did. A Bucklin Dunn Canteen was known all over California, from Mexico to the Northwest Territory.

167

Buck took advantage of every opportunity by offering a free canteen to any manager of any mining or lumber company who allowed him to pitch his men. And pitch he did, returning to Sacramento every five days to get another wagonload of canteens –just like he had on the salt route. To Buck, he had prospered right from the beginning of his journey when he hugged Ever goodbye and told him he'd be back when he was rich. *"I know you will,"* Ever told him.

For the first miles when leaving Golly Springs, heading north to Lexington, Buck balled his eyes out, having left home for the first time on his own. Just as Ever's father had taught his son to survive on the tough streets of Dublin, Ever had instilled a sense of living well in Buck. Living well was something Ever and Buck always had in common, along with a strong work ethic that served them well. Buck was certain that James and Virginia would live a much better life in California, far away from war, slavery, and whites who saw color as an excuse to hate. *"Cowards"* are what Ever called them, *"idiots who pass on their ignorance to each generation."*

***

A creek ran through an abandoned mining camp west of Santa Rosa that led Buck to a beautiful piece of land on 20 acres of Redwoods that reminded him of Golly Springs so much –he bought it for $300.00. Shrewd Bucklin knew that in time he could sell the land for 20 times what he paid for it, because people were moving here from all over the world at an incredible rate. They were every kind of people on earth. There were displaced families from the north and south; deserters were there to get away from a war that all but shattered them; there were young and middle-aged men like Buck with dreams of making it out west, men who refused to get sucked into the war. There

168

were tens of thousands of prospectors and drifters looking for a new start in this new world.

The mining camps were the perfect place for a canteen salesman to hang out, these holding places where Buck's best customers lived and worked. Buck so wished that his family was out here to cash in on this unlimited opportunity. Alarming news of a protracted war coupled with Buck's land, where a house could be built year-'round, made Buck most anxious to send for James and Virginia. He wanted them to escape that southern aristocracy, a society that no war would ever end most whites' belief that people of color were less than them and to be used as property to serve them.

Now, upon hearing from a telegraph operator in Sacramento that a great battle had been fought near Fredericksburg, Buck was determined more than ever to sell his canteens, for he knew that as long as the war continued - Golly Springs was out of business.

That Bloody Angle

L eaving Fredericksburg, James and his driver led the way to Spotsylvania Courthouse, then to a road that led to the place where the big battles were fought over several days in May of *1864*. The Wilderness Campaign would be remembered by veterans on both sides as a place where The Bloody Angle was fought: That's where James was ordered to go. The Rebel officer in charge of the burial detail told James to *"follow your nose to Bloody Angle,"* adding, *"The Yanks got theirs...now get ours. Bring as many as you can in a wagon and cover 'em. They already turned, so best be ready to cover your noses with somethin'."* The officer suddenly laughed as if he was mad, and galloped away on an impressive chestnut stallion.

James's orders were clear: *"Collect all the Rebel dead and bury their remains in Fredericksburg,"* where already thousands were buried in a Confederate cemetery that not long ago were serene pastures near the rich soil beside the Rappahannock, where all roads were mired in mud from heavy rains that could stop entire armies.

The Bloody Angle was a human slaughter pen, an inverted horseshoe where blue and gray bunched up so close in hand-to-hand combat that the dead lay five deep and proved to be worse than the rumors. First off: the smell of death was getting stronger. James ordered the detail to halt so that the men could *"scarf on,"* a term this all colored detail was aware of, all quick to secure cloth coverings over nose and mouth for this most awful but necessary *"death work,"* the veterans called it. One officer who witnessed the carnage at "The Angle" said, *"I never expect to be fully believed when I tell what I say of the horrors of Spotsylvania."* Another said that, *"what ensued was one of those hand-to-hand encounters with clubbed rifles, bayonets, swords and pistols which defies description."*

The mud-caked battle remnant-littered road to The Angle was only wide enough for one wagon at a time to go into the carnage, load a wagon with dead bodies and leave with a load of dead Rebels covered by a large canvas tarp. Then the second wagon could go in as James and his driver rode with a full wagon back to the Confederate cemetery in Fredericksburg for a mass burial. Half the slaves from the detail were already busy digging graves with relatives nearby awaiting that first wagonload of the dead.

To James, it seemed like it took an hour to load his wagon with dead bodies, their mouths and noses covered the whole time –all the way to Fredericksburg. Not a word was spoken by James and his driver, all the while knowing they would have to go back for more loads by the looks of the indescribable carnage. Their hands were stained with dry blood that would wash away, yet the images they beheld would last a lifetime. These were images that only the savagery of this war could reveal for two free black men like James and his driver. These were two men who in the spring of 1864 had not only seen how cruel war is, but rather - how cruel white men can be to each other on such a vast scale.

Hauling body after gruesome body to the wagon they could hear some men calling out or gasping for life way back near the cluttered slaughter pen known as The Bloody Angle, truly the most savage of battles with so much close firing and hand-to-hand fighting to the death. But Jeff Davis had ordered them here. That's really what kept James's driver from running north: the fact that President Davis was known to grant *free man status* to slaves with distinguished service to the Confederacy.

Load after gruesome load in misty fog over 48 hours straight –and the battlefield was cleared of the dead, their body parts left for the local wild hogs that would return soon. James endured by thinking of Virginia, his sweet woman waiting for him at home. He would daydream about their perfect life in their cozy little home so close to Ever, Rebecca, and Dolly. Like these slaughtered heaps of mutilated flesh and bone, he too had a family that cared for him and loved him. And now: *"I'm the last person on earth to see these men before they are buried forever."* That was a thought that kept coming to him and reminding him that every soldier here would never be seen alive again by their family.

James Virginia Golly had been put in charge of identifying the dead…if possible. It was during this period of being *"boss man,"* he would go about the business of searching clothing to see if any identification could be ascribed to the dead soldier in arms. Letters from home, jewelry with inscriptions, names sewn onto clothing; *"Mr. Golly"* was caught off guard by the obvious respect paid by men in the detail who would come to him with any information that might lead a loved one to believe their loved one was at least accounted for. And there would be droves of civilians, mostly older men who brought women of all ages searching for their husbands, sons and brothers.

On more than one occasion, James was overseeing the unloading and quick burial of a dead soldier when a civilian would spot a loved one and come running to claim and retrieve the body. Such finds were welcome by all, since one less body

172

to bury did matter to each and every one of these men assigned to this gruesome work.

Waiting in Fredericksburg

W hat a beautiful day filled with sunshine it was when Everson Golly arrived at a boardinghouse he took by the night on Pitt Street in Fredericksburg, a vacant block from the Rappahannock River. Two and a half years ago the Battle of Fredericksburg was the largest concentration of troops in any Civil War battle, 200,000 combatants. Thirteen thousand Yankee casualties turned Fredericksburg into a National Cemetery site where mostly privates were buried. Perhaps a third of the buried men were identified by a name carved into an ammunition box or haversack somewhere.

Ever found out in Richmond that James was given his freedom and forgiveness of the charges filed against him by Jeff Davis himself if James would lead the burial detail of slaves and instruct them on saving and attaching any way of identifying the dead if possible. James was chosen for this job because he was the only one who could read and write in the detail. Ever was not aware that James had not heard this act of clemency that would certainly aid in the uncertainties going on everywhere.

Ever did not hesitate driving his best pair of mules to Fredericksburg; he was off to find James and bring him home after his service was done with the burial detail. The Confederate cemetery was not far from downtown Fredericksburg. Ever stayed away from the endless stream of

wagons hauling back the dead from The Wilderness. He heard
from a telegraph clerk that the burial detail would be served a
grand meal when the job was finished, a thank you from the
Daughters of the Confederacy. Ever found out while dining at a
tavern downtown that the meal for the burial detail would be
served at the Fredericksburg Grain Depot, a building that has
been out of service since the early days of the war.

Ever went to the old depot and saw the Daughters of the
Confederacy preparing *"for the big feed"* coming in two days –
they hoped.

***

More like three days later was when the last Rebel was
buried under unmarked headstones. The last man found at
Bloody Angle, at the bottom of a stack 5-deep was a man with
no identification on him. James was exhausted physically and
mentally from this incredible experience. He wanted to lie down
on the wagon and sleep for the first time in more than 80 hours;
however, the sight and smell of the wagon's bed changed his
mind.

A Confederate officer thanked James for the work he and his
detail had performed before giving them directions to the old
grain depot. When thorough James asked the officer if he would
sign some statement *"proving I had completed the detail work in
case the private detective pursued me."* The officer told James
that he should secure the statement from Captain Bordon, the
officer who made the offer. On top of that: the officer ordered
James to lead the wagons in the detail to the river, where they
would scrub clean every wagon before returning them to the
Richmond army livery. After that was done they could go to the
depot for their big meal. That meant another 12 hours at least
before James and the men could rest their bodies, let alone their

175

big free meal. Ever had been parked at the grain depot ever since this morning when he heard the burial detail had finished.

It wasn't until 9 P.M. that evening that the haggard detail walked into the depot; they had been delayed a few hours by a nearby skirmish that forced them to halt. Burial details were immune from confiscation, and James let them know that right away. The Union soldiers thought they could intimidate the all-colored burial detail –until James launched into a tirade of words as if he was the great orator Frederick Douglass:

"You men could be punished severely for detaining us. You can be certain of that. We are free men here...burying the dead...without pay...so we may be free to do as we please."

At the grain depot, James found Ever asleep on his wagon bed, the blue and white *Golly Springs* letters faded on the wagon's sides lit by moonlight.   Some of the haggard men of the detail watched James wake Ever, who was elated to see James. James scooped up crystals of salt that were always present on the wagon's bed; he took a few and put them in his mouth, and handed out the rest to some men of the detail who had to be salt depleted, living off lard biscuits and coffee for 5 days.

The men dined on the floor of the old depot, leaning against the four walls. The yellow-orange glow of flickering candles placed on the floor every 10 feet or so by The Daughters of the Confederacy gave the room the appearance of grace and hospitality these men appreciated. Later, James and Ever would talk about how the men were polite and humbled by these women serving them boiled chicken with greens and potatoes, along with good coffee and ginger cookies for dessert. After this fine meal the men were surprised to see a blanket placed in front of each man, another gift for their service. *"Sleep if you can,"* the woman in the gray dress and bonnet told James after

176

informing him that the wagons from the burial detail had indeed been confiscated by the same Union soldiers he encountered earlier.

To Richmond

Besides James and Ever, 25 men from the burial detail rode on the Golly Springs wagon the next morning. They'd been given food and rest thanks to The Daughters of the Confederacy. Most of the way back to Richmond was perilous to say the least, replete with the sounds of war and occasional Rebel yells, causing all the men of the detail to be wary and on edge. There were shots of cannon, infantry skirmishes, and union cavalry on the move that forced the Golly Springs detail off the road several times. Of these men riding in the wagon, only Ever had not seen the cruelty of war up close and personal.

Ever held the reins as James rode beside him, nodding off, as were most of the men behind them. Ever could see in James's eyes that he had seen awful things since leaving Richmond. It was even more apparent when he told James that because of his service his judgment from Mrs. Pemberton would be dismissed. James acted as if he didn't believe any of it.

Rumors flew that Grant was getting ready to tighten his grip on Richmond at Petersburg. Ever told James that he thought they should get Dolly from school and take her home before Derwent was taken over by an army. James agreed and yet both men were wary of having either army stopping them, and forcing them to collect their dead after another battle; for "the butcher" Grant was relentless, sending tens of thousands to early graves on both sides *"until all of Virginia's soil turns red...jus' like it did at Bloody Angle."* Nevertheless, these men believed they would receive "Free Man" status or in James's case, absolution of a debt from Jeff Davis once they returned from their grisly work done for The Confederacy. To the man, they wanted to believe that they would get "official papers" proving such status, so hope was alive as the Golly Springs wagon wheels turned mile after halting mile until darkness came and they camped for the night only seven miles from their destination.

There were rumors of bushwhackers around, civilians and deserters from both sides who were known to storm wagons like this while riding some of the finest horses bred in Virginia. These were the "backwoods men" that used war as an excuse to raid unarmed civilians of their valuables, which included wagons and animals.

This was one perfect evening in May compared to the mud bath the detail endured after The Wilderness. This was the calm after the storm. Most of the men of the detail fell right to sleep on a lush green knoll that hadn't been trampled or burned by war. Two of the eldest and most infirm men of the detail fell off to sleep fast on the wagon bed while James and Ever were awake and talking while leaning against a large oak tree; they were gazing up at the star-filled sky as distant cannon rumbled from Petersburg.

"In Big Lick there's talk about the Yankee cavalry taking the salt mines in Saltville," Ever said.

"When did you hear that?" James was curious.

"Last week Rebel cavalry turned back Sheridan just south of Lexington. Yankee prisoners said they were on the way to Saltville. It's all part of Grant's plan to take Richmond."

"Who do you think will win the war?" James asked.

"I don't know. And I don't see rich people givin' up their slaves till Lincoln's Army makes 'em."

"If the South wins or becomes a separate country I won't raise a family in Virginia," James was certain.

"They won't bother you at Golly Springs," Ever was certain.

"You don't know that for sure. I would not want my children to live in a country where slavery was legal."

"You're not alone. There are lots of folks in Virginia who don't want the South to break away."

"I hear California is a Free State and we could go there and live near Buck," James was hopeful.

"Until we hear from Buck I don't think it's wise to go and try to find him. You know what he said: he's not comin' back till he's rich."

James smiled at the memory of his adventurous brother, then said, "I hope he doesn't come back till this war is over."

Ever agreed and closed his eyes to sleep.

***

An hour before dawn, Ever and James woke all the men and continued on to Richmond. Two of the men had taken off for the North during the night, deciding not to trust Jeff Davis with their freedom. Slaves were still known to be hunted down and returned to their owner even though Lincoln had abolished slavery, yet these two "rabbits" decided to take their chances and high-tail it to Baltimore. The Golly Springs wagon was lighter by three more men when it reached downtown Richmond's constable's office where the detail was formed. Ever and James stood at the head of the line, waiting for the constable to return to confirm the absolution of the judgment against James.

By the time "the man" arrived at his office, and looking hung over from a night of hard drinking –Ever knew they were going to have a problem.

"We need some official proof that the debt has been paid by James and that Mrs. Pemberton has no claim against James and that his wife, Virginia, is free," Ever told the red-eyed constable, whose face showed no sign of competence.

James stepped in when the man's memory failed him.

"I led the burial detail to Fredericksburg. You said I could have the judgment against me by Mrs. Pemberton dropped if I finished the burial detail."

"Oh, Yes, certainly. There was a man here two days ago as I recall inquiring about the runaway owned by Mrs. Pemberton."

"She's my wife now, sir."

"That bounty hunter does not know that James has been absolved from the debt because of his service on the burial detail. That's what you told me, sir," Ever was intense.

"I want proof for my wife. I want Jeff Davis to sign a letter from you stating my service; then I can show it to Mrs. Pemberton, sir."

"I can certainly compose a quick letter now and as far as getting Mr. Davis to sign it…well sir, that's another matter."

"I'd like to take the letter with me," James said.

After the constable gave James his signed letter that Jeff Davis needed to sign to absolve James of the judgment against him, James had the constable write on the letter stating that Virginia Golly is now owned *by James Virginia Golly.* Then, Ever watched James take over.

"Constable, I will sit down with your permission and write out a freedom statement for their service to The Confederacy that each man would petition the President to sign."

Ever escorted each man from the burial detail into the constable's office. Each man gave their name to James, which he in turn printed on the man's letter of freedom that the constable signed and dated, attesting to the man's service completed for The Wilderness burial detail.

Later, outside the constable's office, James told the men that the constable's letter was as good as gold for their freedom. *"A Virginia lawman signed your freedom paper. Jeff Davis is too busy these days to sign anything. But you show that paper to anyone asking for proof and that's your Free Man paper there."*

When Ever and James left the constable's office, they went straight to the Richmond Hotel to see if that bounty hunter had been around. The hotel was closed because Lee's Army had confiscated every provision in Richmond stores. Even though they were hungry and anxious to get home, before heading off to Derwent to pick up Dolly they decided to show Mrs. Pemberton the letter proving Virginia's freedom status. The Golly men agreed that any chance to stop some ruthless bounty hunter from tracking down Virginia was worth taking.

This is War

In need of food and baths, Ever accompanied James up to the Pemberton House front door. James rapped the lion's head on the widow's solid front door. A domestic opened the door and recognized James as the man who took Virginia away and married her. The woman could smell death on his clothes and was obviously repulsed by it.

"May I speak to Mrs. Pemberton regarding Virginia?" James asked her.

"Mrs. Pemberton is not able to receive visitors."

Not wanting to give his only copy of his note from the constable, he asked the woman if she could read his note. She could not. He told her to tell Mrs. P. that the constable signed his name and gave Virginia her freedom because of his service to The Confederacy.

"And tell her that Virginia is my wife now, and we are not to be bothered by any bounty hunter."

***

During their 12-mile ride to Derwent, a Rebel straggler fed up with the deprivations of war, informed Ever that Grant was pushing his troops closer to Richmond by digging in at Petersburg:

183

"Grant and Sherman gonna hook up and starve Old Bobby Lee out of Richmond and burn it down jus' like Vicksburg and Atlanta."

All the way to Derwent James thought about his Virginia, and how the Richmond whites feared that blacks in the city would rise up against them, since more and more were skilled laborers and free to work in factories and other jobs with decent wages.

Richmond was going mad with inflated prices for basic necessities that were six, seven times the normal cost. A pair of socks cost $2.50, and a pound of bacon or coffee were grounds for assault and robbery by the growing number of desperate thugs roaming the capital city. Alarming news that blacks were needed to dig Lee's trenches at Petersburg along with more burial details needed after Lee and Grant fought it out at Cold Harbor and Five Forks –kept James and Ever wary of being forced into labor for the South.

By now there was only enough grain to get the Golly mules home after picking up Dolly. No way were James and Ever going to turn back now, for these were peaceful men like most men of western Virginia whose vast majority of votes against secession had been dismissed by the men of influence and power in the South's most prosperous city, that was now in the throes of a full-blown panic because Grant and Sherman were closing in and leaving half their dead and wounded along the way.

Reaching the school on an otherwise perfect late spring day, Ever found Dolly working at a table with other young women making bandages from dormitory linen that was to be sent to the same hospital Dolly visited the day James was jailed in Richmond. The wounded have been pouring into the city at a deplorable rate ever since Grant took charge of "Lincoln's Army."

Dolly was elated to see Ever, hugging him tight before introducing him to her classmates. She would be packed and ready to go home with all her things in less than an hour, the same time it took James to water and feed the last of the grain to the mules.

"It's immoral and a complete abomination to be stranded here," one of Dolly's classmates complained in her sweet southern drawl to Ever as Dolly hurried to her room to pack.

***

Dolly would hear all about the ghastly work James did for The Confederacy in order to win Virginia's freedom. Knowing the bounty hunter was looking for Mrs. Pemberton's "property," Dolly remained poised and optimistic when she told the men:

"Good. When the bounty hunter comes, we have the proof from the constable that the debt is paid."

This would be the longest ride home for James. Even his perilous voyage across the ocean from Africa paled in comparison to this, for now he was an educated man acutely aware of how cruel and inhumane slavery is after experiencing total freedom inside his adopted family. He knew too well that a loved one could be taken from him and never seen again. And here they were, taking this less traveled road to Golly Springs, each of them successful in their own right in the very heart of America's Civil War.

Ever had already made up his mind: if the North wins –he'll stay at Golly Springs knowing that slavery is over; if the South prevails –he'll move his family out west to California and start a new life with Buck.

Near the end of their journey home it was nightfall when the Golly Springs wagon approached James Creek. Upon crossing the bridge, James was so excited to see his wife that he hopped off the wagon and ran for his house. Inside his home there was no sign of Virginia, and nothing to indicate she had been found and taken away. Hoping she was at the main house –he ran as fast as he could across the Golly land with Ever and Dolly following in the wagon. All he could think of was that Virginia would tell him that if he was gone for the night she would stay with Rebecca since Rebel infantry and cavalry were frequently seen and heard beyond the woods surrounding Golly Springs.

It was late enough for all of them to be in bed, yet the door was unlocked and no candles were lit inside the dark house when James opened the door. He held his breath after calling out, "We're home!" Nothing. His boots hurried over the wood floor to the spare bedroom where he and Buck used to sleep. It was dark and no sign of Virginia or any of her things. Outside Rebecca and Ever's bedroom he called out for his step-mother…and again nothing.

Ever entered his home carrying a lit lantern and Dolly came in behind him carrying one of her bags. Ever noticed that his loaded pistol always hanging high up on a peg…was not there. James's heart was racing when he said to them, "They're gone." Ever remained calm when he told James they must be at Bonham House and "check the animals." Ever hurried to the barn while Ever and Dolly scoured the house. On the floor leading to the kitchen his lamp light revealed scraps of bread and meat on the floor that he knew his wife would not tolerate for an instant. Ever was doing his best to remain calm. Dolly also wanted to believe the women were at Bonham House and held her emotions inside for the sake of these two husbands who were beside themselves.

Dolly wanted to ride in the wagon with Ever; however, Ever knew they needed fresh animals. James ran back from the barn with alarming news, that the animals were all gone. Instantly James saw the same intensity in Ever's eyes he had not seen since the shark attack. Dolly recognized those blazing blue eyes that rescued her and Buck on The Dutchman.

They could see him thinking and followed him right away over to the healing waters that had saved all of them. This was where Ever always went alone to pray, like now when he stopped at the edge of the bubbling water and stared down at the steaming darkness covering his feet. Now James and Dolly flanked him; they waited for him to say what they would do next.

"I'll get the animals fed while you go home and get into some dry clothes," Ever said to James.

"Dry clothes?" James queried.

Ever pushed James into the hot water, tossing a cake of soap at him:

"Get those clothes off and scrub off that death smell. You don't want the women smelling that. We'll pick you up at your house after we feed the animals and ourselves. Dolly will get us fed and bring along what we need."

"Need for what?" James was peeling off his soiled clothes and boots.

"For war," Ever's eyes glowed down at him.

James watched Ever lead the tired mules to the barn after Dolly went inside the house to change clothes. He scrubbed himself from head to toe with Rebecca's lavender soap, a fragrance Virginia always loved. The stench of The Wilderness was killed instantly when submerged in these healing waters that seemed to be giving James all his strength back. There was no more fear in these waters, for he saw the knowing eyes of Dolly that reminded him that Everson Golly would find Rebecca and Virginia and return them home safely.

Meanwhile, soon after lighting a bedside candle in her room, Dolly quickly changed clothes and couldn't help thinking how "ironic and strange" it all seemed if Rebecca and Virginia have been stolen from Ever and James. Then, as Dolly pulled on her work boots upon donning her roughest outfit she only wore when horseback riding and barn work, she reminded herself how she's been planning on telling the whole family tonight that she was quitting school and going to California to find Buck. At Derwent she researched the best route for a woman traveling alone from Virginia to California. It was not the same route Buck had taken. Instead of a wagon she would take a stagecoach from Big Lick to Saint Louis, then a steamboat to Kansas City, whereupon she would take a stagecoach across Kansas and into the Southwest until reaching California forty days later. But now this. She couldn't leave home now if half her family was missing.

Dolly also went into the dark kitchen; with the aid of her candle she too saw the food scraps on the floor that fastidious Rebecca would never leave behind. She agreed with Ever: If this is so –this is war.

One Long Surprise

O nly the wealthy sailed on this clipper ship named *The Culpepper*. Most of the passengers were the lucky men who struck it rich in the goldfields in California. These were such men returning home to their native South, to buy up land and property that was selling for bargain prices by sellers hungry for real U. S. greenbacks.

Each passenger had his own private quarters, a tiny cabin with one meal delivered once a day, along with 5 gallons of fresh water delivered every week over eight weeks for $600.00. Sailing thousands of miles around South America and up to Virginia, Bucklin Dunn wanted to avoid the great American Civil War uncertainties and arrive in Virginia far more rested, preferring to take his chances on Petersburg Road, a road he knew far better than most men manning the trenches on both sides. Buck read books he'd bought in busy San Francisco for twelve hours a day on his voyage home. For hours a day he walked around the deck, keeping his legs strong. He had first heard of The Culpepper while in Sacramento over a year ago while in the throes of making his fortune with his *Bucklin Dunn* line of canteens and cooking wares he sold to thousands of prospectors on the road right off his wagon.

Unsure of exactly when Grant would take Richmond, Buck was confident that the Union bulldog general would whip Bobby Lee sooner than later. He'd heard of Grant and Lee's extensive trenches south of Petersburg and the siege that would eventually starve Lee's men, forcing them to abandon the Rebel capital. And he also heard the men in California, his customers, a collection of deserters, stragglers and shiftless men of all types who believed to a man that blacks whether slaves or free would never be equal to whites in any of the Rebel States. It didn't take a mental giant to realize that these men were ignorant, and that if any of them knew his brother, James –they would sing a different tune.

Now Bucklin Dunn was doing what his father promised his mother: to return home when he was able to provide for them. Buck never did find his father in the tens of thousands of faces of dreamers he'd met in California. In Buck's fourteen hundred days since leaving home, every one of those days he wished his brother was with him, selling with him every day in the golden hills of California. He saw in waking dreams his brother's quick-big smile and their competitive spirits soaring by wanting to beat the other for the day, for the week, whenever. Happy memories of he and James competing for who paid for their meal that day; for who loaded the winner's wagon for next week's run; or, who would be the loser and stable the winner's animals when returning home at the end of the week. It was all such glorious fun, and Buck yearned to have his brother's company again, in California, far away from plantations, iron leggings, and a thousand other deplorable things they had witnessed together.

Near his destination, sailing through darkness up the Atlantic off the South Carolina coast and while in his cabin resting, Buck recalled the time he and his brother shared the same bed not long after Ever and Rebecca were married. Rebecca had come into the room to blow out their bedside candle and she heard the boys crying with their faces hidden under the covers. The boys heard their new step-mother/teacher asking them why they were crying. Buck kept his head under the covers and told her they missed their parents. Rebecca sat on the side of their bed and had them look at her. They did.

"There are times I miss my parents. My mother died when I was about your age. What always helped me was that we'd all be together in God's Heaven when we leave this earth."

"After we die?" Buck asked.

"Yes."

"But I want to see them now when I'm here." Buck whined.

"I don't," James mumbled. "I don't want to see them as slaves. It would be too sad to see."

They could see Rebecca begin to cry. That's when James said:

"Don't feel so sad. I know God brought Ever to me on that vast ocean…just as I know He brought you to Ever to be our mother. This is how we can live our lives now here at Golly Springs."

She bid them both good night and blew out their candle after telling the boys she loved them. When Rebecca left their room, Buck whispered to James that when he was on The Dutchman just before his mother died, his mother told him that she prayed that our lives would be one long surprise.

"I forgot she told me that. And I do want to live like my life is one long surprise."

"I think we should start living that way," James agreed.

Lying on his cabin bed as his ship sailed north along the South Carolina coast, Buck closed his eyes and recalled with fondness how his life has indeed been one long surprise, just as his mother prayed it would be.

Where God Lives

Off-boarding at Norfolk in early July of 1864, it was obvious now that this was a busy Yankee port taken over by Grant's Army. Before any passenger could step foot on Virginia soil The Culpepper was searched for any contraband that could aid Lee's dwindling army. Buck remembered this being a listless atmosphere compared to today, where rather than slaves working at a desultory pace –they were now at work like one human buzz saw, knowing they were working for decent wages and freedom was at hand as President Lincoln said.

Carrying an expensive bag in each hand, it was obvious to Buck that even a rich man could not get transportation around this place, for every animal was needed for Grant's siege at Petersburg and not to be eaten by Lee's starving army. So— Buck started walking, taking the same route Ever had taken when first landing on American soil. This time Bucklin Dunn was a shrewd businessman who knew how to overcome deprivations even in a war-torn environment as in eastern Virginia.

In Suffolk he waited for his first opportunity that came along: An old man riding bareback on an even older chestnut mare, was convinced to walk home for two twenty-dollar gold pieces. Loping at a man's walk, Buck rode to the southern fringe of Petersburg with each of his bags tied together by a piece of hemp and hanging over the front flank of the old horse.

The road was one dust cloud of supplies headed for Grant's Army dug in and waiting for Lee's next move at Petersburg. When Buck reached Petersburg Road he was told by a Union sentry that he could go no further, only back the way he came. The timing could not have been worse for using the only decent road that led all the way home. Another soldier told the well-dressed young man that Grant wanted Petersburg Road clear in case Bobby Lee made a run for it and high-tailed his army west to the mountains of western Virginia. No way did Buck want to return to Suffolk. War or no war, Bucklin Dunn was not about to wait around for Grant or Lee to make a move. Confidence was a trait he gained with experience on his salt route and selling thousands of prospectors his products out west; all that experience made him bolder whenever obstacles came his way now.

A few years back, in the early months of the war when General Lee began his string of beating every Union general that faced him in battle, Buck was then new to California and had met a man who claimed to have shook Marsh Robert's hand. *"Right at his front door,"* the man boasted. The man's story was so interesting to Buck: The man was from Boston; he said he bought a Confederate private's uniform taken from the field after Bull Run; he rode his horse to Maryland, where he could safely change into that Rebel uniform. He claimed he rode all the way to Richmond just to shake the hand of a man who was destined for greatness. He told Buck how his plan was to go to Lee's home at 707 East Franklin Street in Richmond when the general was home for one of his brief visits. Since Buck knew of the Lee home, upon passing it by every time he worked Franklin Street; and even though it was one of the few homes that was

194

never a customer on his route –he found the man's claim credible. The man described the Greek-Revival brick town house perfectly and said, *"I knocked on the general's door, removed my hat, and there he be. I forgot my Southern accent and asked if I could please just shake his hand. When I saw his right hand comin' toward me I looked into his eyes and saw a light comin' out so bright. I let go his hand, thanked him and walked away as if I'd just met God himself."* He told Buck he didn't wash his right hand for the longest time because he saw where God lived and shook his hand.

Now: Buck too must find a place to change, into the Yankee-blue private's uniform he bought in San Francisco. Buck reasoned like the man from Boston had reasoned: that a private wasn't expected to know much or explain much. Buck would wait until nightfall, when he could pass by a new sentry that hadn't seen him earlier. This way he could make his way to the left flank of Grant's entrenched troops, change back into safer civilian clothes and make his way home, saving himself at least two days of arduous travel well south of Petersburg in a paranoid country where every stranger was a target. Buck was certain he did not want to be a target for some Rebel sympathizer lurking in the woods somewhere. That was his plan.

That night it began to rain and did not let up by the time Private Golly, a volunteer from California (if anyone asked), rode up to a new sentry on the east end of Petersburg Road where Grant's Army was stacked 30-men deep for 16 miles east to west. The road west was clogged with wagons and soldiers because *"something big"* was planned to happen soon, therefore security was extremely heavy and wary of Rebel spies. Three sentries made Buck dismount while they went through his bags thoroughly.

"What's your brigade?" one sentry asked Buck.

195

"I have none. I came as a volunteer from California to return home to western Virginia."

"So, you thought you'd put on a uniform and think you can ride on down the road?"

"That's about right. I was going to change back into my clothes once I got past the line and ride home."

"I'm putting you under arrest as a Rebel spy."

Upon hearing these words, Buck wished he had taken the long way home, away from this last stand by Bobby Lee; and, now he realized that putting on a uniform was not a smart thing to do. Within an hour, Private Dunn was in handcuffs and leg irons, seated cross-legged at the bottom of a muddy trench with a few other men in one kind of trouble or another. His bags and old mare were taken somewhere, yet Buck was smart enough to hide his money, some two thousand dollars, sewn into his underwear.

The other men with him were thieves and stragglers; they enlightened the imposter private in the clean uniform, warning him of what was coming: "Grant's diggin' a tunnel from here to Lee's trenches. He's gonna blow it all to hell and break Lee's line."

"Why are you telling me this?" Buck asked the prisoner.

"Cause that's where we's headed."

"Where?" Buck was confused.

"To dig Grant's tunnel. Every man they find like us they throw into that tunnel. They don't trust the likes of us, so they'll make us dig and haul out dirt for sixteen hours a day."

196

"But I'm with no regiment. I'm a volunteer," Buck protested.

"Well, you just volunteered to be a mole for U. S. Grant," the other men laughed with him.

Without Virginia

It had been a week since Ever and James and Dolly found Rebecca walking back from Bonham House...without Virginia. A roving band of Confederate deserters, renegades and raiders in tattered Rebel uniforms, swooped into Golly Springs on horseback from the mountains way back in western Virginia. They'd steal all the animals and every black person they saw, taking them to the same consumer: Lee's hungry and tired men caught in Grant's vice grip. The hardships caused by war on Rebel soil ravaged the South compared to Lincoln's well fed and supplied army. These same men who took Virginia operated freely because they were an organized party of wounded former Rebel cavalry, men who would roam all over Virginia confiscating animals to feed Lee's starving men. Then, they started kidnapping free men and women of color that they would in-turn sell for as much as $500.00 in order to buy much needed food and supplies to keep going.

James was beside himself and could not help but wish that it had been the bounty hunter that took his Virginia; at least then he would know exactly where to find his wife. It was Rebecca who talked James into calming his emotions by telling James that the men who took Virginia were not rough with her. Since Rebecca and Virginia knew nothing about the bounty put out for Virginia, both of the women assumed that Virginia would be taken back to Pemberton House by these men who took both of them, leaving

Rebecca at Bonham House after Rebecca told them she was a teacher, and to *"please not damage our schoolhouse."*

"They said they wanted food and animals. When they saw Virginia tending her garden, they told her to come with them. They had us ride in the carriage to Bonham House, driving off with Virginia after leaving me there."

"How do you know they weren't bounty hunters?" James asked his distraught step-mother.

"Bounty hunters don't travel in groups," Ever answered for his wife with a sense of finality that James had to agree with. "We'll rest the animals then go after her," Ever told James, who wanted to head back to Richmond right away. Then: Ever went right at James, into those same brown circles of fear he hadn't seen since he first saw the terrified little African boy at sea. It was clear to Ever that he must persuade James to rest here at Golly Springs. Personal energy was important to Everson Golly, for he knew his limitations and when to rest when a big task was before him. And this was going to be a monumental task, tracking down Virginia in a starving city under siege, where a man's wife could be taken and sold to any buyer for any reason.

***

For two days and before leaving for Richmond, the Golly men recovered their strength by soaking in the salubrious waters for hours at a time. Ever talked openly to James about whether to leave their only weapon with Rebecca, the same musket her father had given him. Since Dolly would now stay at home with Rebecca, Ever and James made sure the women were familiar with loading and firing Herb Bonham's gift.

"What if we need it to make someone give us back Virginia?" James argued.

199

Ever satisfied James by telling him they would leave the musket here and secure a weapon in Richmond if needed. Ever planned on not needing any weapon to bring his daughter-in-law home safely.

On the third morning since finding Virginia gone –Ever and James left home with fresh mules and enough food to sustain them for a week. Deserters and desperate war-weary Rebels were leaving the Petersburg trenches by the score every day and walking back home by the hundreds every week. Grant's stranglehold on Lee was proving to be as effective as Vicksburg had been out west. It was just a matter of time before Lee surrendered the capital of the Confederacy in order to get his troops supplied the way any army needed to be in order to keep fighting.

The kidnappers had missed confiscating a full barrel of salt in the Golly barn that now rode on the bed of the Golly Springs wagon along Petersburg Road. Ever thought perhaps they could use their last barrel of salt to bargain for information that would lead them to finding Virginia.

At the western edge of Grant's left flank, Yankee sentries stopped and inspected their wagon –as every civilian wagon was. There was no getting into Richmond now from the west or the south; Grant had the area buttoned up so tight that even Confederate deserters couldn't return to their homes without being captured and sent north to prison.

As with Buck, there was nobody getting into Richmond since only Grant's Army had access to Petersburg Road. Now Ever and James could only go south –or back the way they came. Their wagon and team would be confiscated by the army if they did not "*decide quick.*" Ever had no choice, he had to turn around his wagon and head back home, "*since there's no way to get into Richmond.*"

James had Ever pull over to the side of the road since James wanted to get his gear and head for Richmond on foot.

"You going to swim across the James River?" Ever asked James.

"If I have to," James answered while stuffing provisions into a tow sack.

"We're not even sure she's in Richmond," Ever said.

"Whatever, I can't stay home or wait for Grant or Lee to move while my wife's God knows where."

"What if she's not in Richmond, James? She could be anywhere but Richmond."

"I have to find out," James said after hopping down from the wagon bed and slinging the sack of provisions over his shoulder.

Ever was torn between leaving his wagon here and going with James or heading home; he knew if he left his wagon behind it would be taken. He watched James walk away from the wagon until:

"Wait, James!"

James waited, and was determined to resist any talk about not going after Virginia now, since he saw that Ever wasn't getting things from the wagon to take with him. Ever stood before James and told him that he can't get back the animals they took and that this is all they have. Ever continued:

"There's a place south of here, the Kettle Plantation. I can leave the team there for a while. We can find a way into Richmond on foot…maybe."

James nodded that it sounded like a plan he liked and they walked back to the wagon.

***

The Kettle Plantation was a good customer on the salt route. Virginia Golly had even been to the modest farm several times with Rebecca when they delivered books for the children of slaves. One of the altruistic Kettle women had been home-schooling her children and wanted to include the children of their slaves, *"who are bound to be freed by Lincoln, and should know how to read and write when they leave us."* Mrs. Kettle loved Rebecca. So Ever knew that this was a good place to keep his wagon and team while he went on foot with James to find a way into Richmond.

James did his best to feed his mind positive images and words –as Ever had taught him to do; however –he kept seeing his beloved wife in the hands of those Rebel scavengers that James was now certain would've entered Richmond from the north. It was Ever who insisted on taking their chances with the Yankee blue line since Rebels and jittery Richmond civilians were known to fire on any men trying to get into Richmond – unless they were bringing much-needed supplies for Lee's gaunt army.

About the time the Kettle Plantation came into view, Ever told James, "Whatever comes, we stay together." James gave a positive nod, knowing in his heart that if any man could help him find his Virginia…Everson Golly was the best man to be leading the way.

Make It So

About the same time Ever and James had walked twenty miles east on Petersburg Road, some 8 hours of slogging through mud and animal dung –both Buck and Virginia had literally walked away from their captors…all the way home. Virginia didn't make it to Richmond; five miles from the city during a rainstorm, she managed to slip away from the gang of men who were more concerned with Yankee cavalry all around them. Having been forced to leave home without her shoes, Virginia's feet were in bad shape until Rebecca and Dolly helped her into the healing waters of Golly Springs.

It was but a few hours later when a dirty and haggard Private Dunn appeared at the front door of the house he helped build. He looked like he'd been digging a tunnel for twelve days in the stinking uniform he'd worked and slept in for nearly a fortnight without a bath. Since his bags were "confiscated," after soaking and shaving his hairy face in the springs, he was grateful to wear his brother's clothes that Virginia gave him. Dolly wanted to know all about his life in California since leaving home nearly four years ago. Later that evening as his clean uniform dried outside in the July breezes, he kept his family spellbound by his captivating description of the land he bought *"along the edge of giant trees hundreds of years old in soil worth more than gold."*

He told them of his riches and how he got it with hard work and constancy. Then he lobbied for them to come to California to live on the land he bought for all of them.

"We have to get far away from the South's eternal unwillingness to put slavery behind them."

Virginia knew well what Buck was talking about and could only nod her head in agreement as Dolly voiced the Golly opinion beautifully: "Yes, there is no law that changes people. It's going to take many generations to change hearts and minds about skin color and real equality."

"Yes," Rebecca agreed emphatically, adding, "but Everson Golly will never leave Golly Springs."

"Perhaps he will now after Rebels have come here and just took Virginia like some piece of property they don't and will never respect."

Dolly agreed with her brother and was so elated to see him – it gave her the impetus to tell Rebecca that she was quitting Derwent, "that aristocratic school that breeds a new generation of educated snobs."

Dolly went on to proclaim that she would go with Buck back to California and "leave the South to its own demise."

"Grant's gonna try to break Lee's line by blowin' it up. He's got hundreds of men diggin' this secret tunnel. I was underground for days, not even sure how many. Like Virginia, I just walked away. If James and Ever are trying to get into Richmond…they'll end up digging Grant's tunnel too."

"Why's that?" Virginia was alarmed.

"They're putting every man to work, north or south, free or not, until it's finished. My Yankee uniform got me in the tunnel. When I left they were making every able-bodied man in the army or not dig that tunnel."

"But James is not a slave," Virginia protested to her brother-in-law.

"I know. But he's young and strong and Grant's got his mind made up to take Richmond like he did Vicksburg."

"What do we do now?" Rebecca asked Buck.

"I'll get some rest, put on that uniform and try to find 'em," Buck yawned.

"You said you would come back…and you did," Dolly smiled at her tired brother.

Buck had fallen off to sleep fast in his old room as the Golly women prayed together, asking God to make it so James and Ever returned home safely to see that Buck has returned home to them at last.

Dangerous Times To Be Alive

Bucklin Dunn was now a rich man and could certainly find and buy a horse in Big Lick; however, after being on Petersburg Road and upon having the old mare taken by Yankee sentries –he would have to walk. Since leaving the tunnel detail he'd been impressed by the amount of desperation he'd seen in the eyes of men whether north or south. Spooked eyes were everywhere, all moving with this reeking smell of total resignation as if there was no place to get away from war.

In hindsight, as Buck left the next morning in his clean uniform, he realized the blue uniform he was wearing had saved his life several times, since many would have slit his throat if he hadn't changed out of the fancy clothes he'd worn off-boarding The Culpepper in Norfolk.

Death and survival were everywhere on this dirt-rutted road that would eventually run into Grant's left flank. The stench of dead horses and mules, their carcasses with huge chunks cut out of their maggot-infested remains were everywhere. Buck swore to himself he'd never stoop to such desperate measures when he reached the same men in blue who turned James and Ever south in their wagon. This time his worn uniform got him past the Yankee guards as he was allowed to continue his way along a road that had been transformed into absolute chaos and destruction.

Every step was hopeful that there was time to reach Ever and James before the detonation under the Rebel trenches of Lee's dwindling yet tenacious haggard men hanging on for a cause that was slipping further and further away. *Would Grant's men over-run the tattered troops in butternut and gray and take Richmond after the explosion?* Buck wondered, along with a hundred thousand other men in blue sworn to secrecy. Knowing how easy it was for him to be forced into the tunnel, he also knew it would not be possible for Ever and James to escape the same tunnel detail.

***

By dusk Buck had made it to the same holding area where he was shackled and forced to work on the secret tunnel. Except this time there were no men waiting to be used like human moles –so he waited—until he fell off to sleep, using his tow sack of provisions as a pillow. There was no getting good rest here, for sniper shots from sharpshooters on both sides had increased markedly since he was in this same trench last week. On each side of him, men in blue were thick as flies for as far as he could see. The smell of this collective mass was like one stinking dog, the kind of mongrel you either throw into the river or shoot it and throw it into a ditch like this. Either way, Bucklin Dunn had to know if Ever and James had been put to work in the tunnel as part of a thousand-man fire drill passing a 30-pound bucket of Virginia earth and rock every ten seconds 'round the clock.

These are hard times to be alive, Buck said inwardly as he made his way along the trench toward the tunnel entrance, hoping to find James and Ever now before all hell broke loose...and soon. Something about the increased restiveness

Buck saw in the older veterans, who normally talked and joked with a bored kind of weariness that was absent now, replaced by this inchoate sense of impending doom coming…and soon. This change of mood and atmosphere closer to the tunnel caused Buck to talk to every man he could along the trench.

"When's the big boom?" Buck asked a wily veteran who always had a flask of whiskey Buck would sip now and then to help him sleep after a 16-hour shift in the tunnel.

"Sooner than later I expect," the old grizzled veteran warned.

This alarmed Buck, for he believed there was more time until the tunnel reached the Rebel line.

"Isn't General Burnside's Ninth Corps goin' in right after it blows?" Buck asked.

"Yer lookin' at us," the veteran drawled and grinned without a tooth in his mouth.

"Tonight?" Buck had to ask.

"That's the scuttle. Could go any minute."

Buck was surprised at how he felt so overwhelmed at being in possibly the exact spot at the perfect time when Grant could begin taking Richmond, the biggest prize the North could get –as long as Lee's Army of Northern Virginia came with it. He thought: *It would be like Lee taking Washington, and here I am on the front lines.* But then he always came back to the same place of neutrality, unable to take up arms against any side. "*Where are Ever and James?*" he kept asking himself while walking a thousand yards in trenches where Burnside's men were forming for one massive assault right after the explosion. But then: Buck saw what looked like an entire division of

Federal black soldiers moving toward the same entrenchments as one stealthy mass of blue. Seeing all the black soldiers in new uniforms made Buck realize that he was sandwiched between something really big about to happen.

Buck knew that he couldn't leave now if he wanted to. And he knew that if he told them now that he was not a soldier –he'd be shot as a spy on sight. One blue mass readied five thousand shining bayonets then huddled down for hell to erupt, forcing Buck to stay in the trench and take his place with the rest of Burnside's Corps, a collection of veteran white men who for the most part did not want any other sector breaking the door down to Richmond…especially *"a bunch of black Billy Yankees."*

The reality of race was stretched to the limit when these black soldiers were ordered into the trench with Burnside's men. Buck saw the anger and heard the grumbling protests of these veterans who wanted all the glory. But then: it seemed to dawn on every man in Burnside's Corps at once that these fresh black troops recently freed by Lincoln could be sacrificed by slaughter if Lee was waiting for their charge. Either way, the rumors that flew up and down the lines on both sides were true: Grant was digging a tunnel; and, nobody knew for certain when or what was coming. The men knew that the mine was ready to detonate, filled with 320 kegs of gunpowder totaling eight thousand pounds placed just 20 feet under the Confederates trenches 500 feet away with T-shaped wings each going out along the Rebel line for 75 feet.

Buck spent the next four hours curled up in a ball, trying to get some rest with the rest of Burnsides' men. The Ninth Corps was discreetly awakened near 4 A.M. and Bucklin Dunn was resigned to charge the Rebel line with the Ninth Corps. If he didn't –he'd be shot as a deserter by any one of these tough veterans fixing bayonets, ready for close combat. Buck carried no weapon and didn't want one. The realization that he could be killed in this man-swarm just because he was here in a Yankee uniform --instantly dried his mouth and caused his hands to tremble. *"I'm not a soldier,"* his mind kept telling him as veterans who had survived the "the butcher's" battles prepared for another blood bath.

Then: the old vet from the mine, the only man in blue who knew his story, moved over to be next to the young California businessman.

"You can't go in with us unarmed," he said into Buck's fear-filled blue eyes, with eyes the color of war, a yellowish-brown aged beyond years with red veins visible in the July moonlight.

"I can't just leave. They'll shoot me as a deserter," Buck confided to the vet.

He watched the man remove a derringer from inside his boot and gave it to Buck with his words:

"You got one shot. Best use it if obliged. These are dangerous times to be alive," he nodded.

Buck took the derringer, nodding as if to thank the old Pennsylvania coal miner, one of hundreds who had helped dig the tunnel.

Soon the order was barked for Burnside's men to make way for Lincoln's colored troops, who would be the first to assault the Rebel line. In the confusion of grumbling over the last ditch change in positions, Buck was able to see that he was now part of this war and one of the spooked faces of the young who faced the prospect of dying for the rich, those invisible men who profit from war's machinery and blood yet remain far removed from harm. *"Why should these men die? And why*

210

can't we deny these men who profit from war by refusing to fight and support war in any form whatsoever?" These were the thoughts on Bucklin Dunn's mind.

Up close, Buck could now see and hear the united faith of the colored Federal troops praying together, versus the solitary and private prayer from the white soldier. He had learned from his sister-in-law at the family dinner table: *"We must have faith in order to survive every day of our lives. White folks go to church to pray on Sunday; we pray together all the time."*

Now it was Buck's time to pray, for the earth blew up, making a sound so horrific that it sent every man face-down to the rumbling earth while clods of dirt and rock fell from the sky like a Tennessee hailstorm, pelting the earth for a thousand yards in all directions. In pitch-black darkness the moaning and cries of the Rebel wounded began and could be heard above the shouting of men on both sides as the colored division was ordered forward, bayonets fixed, their "butcher" ordering them to the crater that was 170 feet long, 120 feet wide and 30 feet deep. 278 Confederates had been instantly killed by the explosion, some of their body parts landing on blue uniforms.

Then: Burnside's troops were ordered forward, far behind the colored troops who were caught and trapped inside the crater, shot down like fish in a barrel. There were so many Rebels walking around dazed and confused, their eardrums bleeding from the concussion of the blast. Men were surrendering here and there; men with horrific wounds caused by the explosion were everywhere.

Burnside's men tried to move through a gap the explosion caused; however –the Rebels were waiting for them, causing five times the casualties that the explosion caused. The repulse of the

Ninth Corps was so complete that General Burnside was relieved of his command.

Take Me Home

Bow-legged Ozzie was on his rounds going from stall to stall in the Richmond Livery when the explosion went off. "My Lord, have mercy on us all. General Grant is blowin' up the world!" the old livery man whined while his weak legs carried him to the stall where two of his old customers had been staying since walking around Grant's right flank. The Golly men had covered some forty miles of perilous roads east then north, finally finding a safe crossing of the James River that Ever knew well that was not far from North Kent. Every day since arriving, they spent their time scouring downtown Richmond looking for Virginia Golly. Every night they would fall off to sleep in this safe haven that Ozzie called *"my home."*

Ever and James heard the explosion, yet stayed in the warmth of the bed made of straw that Ozzie prepared and reserved for two of his favorite customers.

"You must be mighty tired to sleep through that," the old man smiled down into the sleep-groggy eyes he revealed with his lantern. "Grant's knockin' on Richmond's door and Lincoln's gonna free us all!" he laughed. Within seconds, a loud pounding on the livery's locked door caused the tired guests to get to their feet while Ozzie sauntered off to investigate who was making *"such a ruckus at this hour."*

Ever and James could hear the frenetic voices of men and Ozzie's protestations until the livery doors were opened wide and half-starved Confederate soldiers in tattered rags began pouring into the livery taking every horse and parked wagon as their caretaker stood by helplessly. The soldier in charge of the men took Ozzie's lantern and came over to Ever and James demanding to know *"their business here."*

"We're looking for my daughter-in-law. We believe she's in Richmond."

"We need wagons to move prisoners," the soldier drawled, holding the lantern up to their faces as his men were in a state of panic, hitching horses to wagons as Ozzie feared what his boss and customers would say upon returning and finding the livery gutted. Ever asked the soldier in charge what the big explosion was.

"Grant's comin'," the man drawled in a relaxed tone that belied the commotion going on all around them.

Outside the livery it was still dark and a full-blown panic was underway. Men and wide-eyed horses were flying about in a swirling maelstrom of flight the Golly men had never seen the likes of. They stood with Ozzie, who was beside himself bemoaning his future when an officer on a magnificent black stallion stopped in front of the livery and with pistol in hand ordered the three civilians to "get along to Libby Prison to help with the transport of Yankee prisoners!"

For the half-mile of tramping on sore feet on the brick streets of downtown Richmond, Ozzie bemoaned his plight every step; it wasn't until they reached the entrance of the heavily guarded prison that a string of ambulances wagons parked outside the adjoining hospital began rolling past a growing cluster of civilians who'd been ordered here as well. As wagon after wagon hurried past them, the same officer ordered the last wagon to "Halt!" Then, pistol drawn, he ordered every man onto the wagon, which included the trio from the livery. Fearing the man's sense of urgency, Ever and James hopped onto the wagon and helped Ozzie onto the bed of the last ambulance before it rattled on, destined for the trenches of Petersburg.

***

By the time the wagons reached the Confederate line in Petersburg –the morning sun had been up for an hour, revealing the 30-foot-deep crater caused by the explosion. A cease-fire was on in order to remove the dead and wounded from the crater; most of whom were the black soldiers in blue who were slaughtered like fish in a barrel when Rebels fired down into the crater after the hated black Yankees had rushed into and soon found themselves trapped with no cover or means of escape.

Of the Richmond civilian men forced into the ambulance detail, Ever and James and old Ozzie were but a few who volunteered to go into the crater with the Union detail assigned to this grisly task of removing the dead and wounded. To James, this was far worse than his detail at The Bloody Angle in The Wilderness, for many of the men were of his color and yet alive and calling out in anguish from hideous wounds that few if any could survive. Everson was the only white man from either side willing to remove the dead or wounded black soldiers from the crater, an inhumane sight of prejudice that repulsed him even more than his gruesome work on The Dutchman.

For hours the Golly men and old Oz assisted the Union soldiers of color, toiling with the removal of men dead and alive, hauling them out of the crater. The work was so exhausting, compounding it with no fresh water that the trio collapsed into a

215

Rebel trench, missing their ride back to downtown Richmond. Sooner than later the trio was awakened by the sound of cannon announcing the end of the cease fire. Ever realized then that they better get away before they were forced to man one of Granny Lee's trenches or used for any more labor needed by a starving, ragged army that James thought doomed by comparison to the healthy-looking troops in blue he'd seen gawking down into the crater during the cease fire. When trying to slip away – no such luck. The same officer who ordered them here at gunpoint, spotted the trio and ordered them to drive a wagonload of wounded Rebels back to the hospital in downtown Richmond.

Again they were forced to bear the sounds of mortally wounded men, some dying on the way to the hospital. With no water to give these pleading men, Ever, holding the reins, called out to every human in sight asking for water –to no avail.

Welcome shade from the afternoon sun finally came upon reaching the familiar buildings of downtown Richmond where once-prospering businesses lined both sides of Richmond Avenue, and now reduced to hollow shells abandoned with entire storefronts missing and used for firewood to sustain Marsh Robert's tattered army.

Up ahead the road was clogged with at least a hundred Yankee prisoners taken after Burnside's charge after the explosion. Their Rebel captors would butt and bash these men in blue with their muskets to move the prisoners over so that the ambulance could pass by these "*Yankee scoundrels*" of U. S. Grant, who were despised by every man and woman who cast eyes upon them. To these loyal Richmond civilians, they were looking at the devils that killed their brothers, sons, and husbands…and could not be more detested for the hardships they endure.

James could see their complete resignation, their waning faith that Marsh Robert would prevail against Lincoln's vast armies and resources that were mocking their own tattered army as these clean-shaven soldiers in their new blue uniforms and boots, footwear that would soon be removed upon arrival at Libby Prison and forwarded to the ragged Rebels manning the Petersburg trenches.

Then: the same officer that had ordered them to "the crater" spurred his stallion after a young prisoner who'd bolted from the line and ran for the river, only to be shot in the back by the officer and left in plain view for the others contemplating such a move. Moments earlier, Bucklin Dunn had been talking to the man who now bled an ever-growing pool around his prostrate body. The dead man had been talking to Buck, muttering that he would never be "*Johnny Reb's prisoner*" right before he made his run for the river. Buck had thoughts about giving the man his derringer he'd been given right before their charge after the explosion, a single-shot weapon he'd hidden inside his waistline pocket just before he was captured with these men of Burnside's Ninth Corps.

Just then: Buck saw his brother and Ever driving a wagon of wounded Rebels past him; before they were out of hearing distance:

"Salt Man!" Buck called out to them, a name they'd all been called a thousand times on their salt route. Both Ever and James turned back to the voice that waved his hat above the group of Yankee prisoners.

"It's Buck," James said before jumping down from the moving wagon before Ever could say anything.

The prisoners continued on their forced march to the looming massive prison just beyond the hospital. Before a Rebel guard could push James away with the length of his musket there were quick words exchanged between the reunited brothers:

"What are you doing here?" James asked.

"Looking for you! Virginia sent me!" Buck flashed his puckish grin as the guard pushed James away.

James ran up ahead to catch up with Ever, who was now parked and waiting in line to unload the Rebel wounded at the front entrance of the hospital.

"My God, is it really him?" Ever queried James when he returned to the ambulance and now Ozzie was seated between them on the buckboard.

"Yes, he came looking for us! And he said Virginia is home!"

"Really?" Ever exclaimed, elated along with James as Ozzie very much wanted to go back to the livery.

Energy instantly returned to the Golly men, who hadn't eaten or had any water all day. They turned back to watch the line of prisoners in blue move past them; they stared back at Buck, who they hadn't seen or even heard from in years. Ever waved back at Buck, who looked fit and filled out like a grown man. Both Ever and James reasoned that Buck was wearing a Union uniform in order to get as close as possible to Richmond.

Ozzie held the reins of the ambulance wagon during the unloading of the wounded Rebels that Ever and James carried on stretchers into the crowded hospital that held more suffering than any battlefield James had seen. The Golly men talked discreetly about how they could get Buck out of that prison. Any plan seemed too dangerous after seeing the dead prisoner lying in a pool of blood after his escape attempt. There would be no explaining to anyone that Buck was not a real soldier; that he just happened to be wearing a Yankee uniform when he was captured after the failed assault on Granny Lee's trenches after the explosion. Getting Buck out of that prison fortress seemed impossible considering the state of panic the whole city was in. But then, Ever had an idea that he conveyed to James discreetly:

"Remember when we delivered the salt to the hospital, Dolly had told us she went into the prison basement without seeing a soul?"

James remembered, and Ever continued amidst the calamity going on around them:

"In the hospital kitchen, that man would remember us if we called on him to see how his salt supply is holding up. I say we go see him, and at least if we are caught in the prison we have a man who can verify who we are."

Outside, loading another wounded soldier on the blood-stained stretcher, James had another idea, yet he had to wait until the next wounded man was carried inside, not wanting the Rebel to overhear.

***

Ever liked James's idea better, a plan James was not able to tell Ever until the last wounded man was carried into the hospital's crowded holding area. They stood at the back of the ambulance with Ozzie at the reins as blood dripped from the human cargo onto the dark brick street. Two dead Rebels remained on the ambulance bed when James revealed his idea.

Ever paused to think over the discreet scheme James had revealed, not wanting to involve the old livery man. It sounded more dangerous to Ever than his idea and they'd have to be more patient. Ever admitted that, "It might just work. Let's do it."

Ever told Ozzie to drive them to the livery where they could "wash off the blood" on the ambulance bed before taking the two dead Rebels to the Confederate cemetery a few miles north of the James River District. While James and Ozzie fetched water from the livery trough in back, Ever removed the uniform from one dead Rebel and put it on in one of the many empty dark stalls. James helped him wash off the blood best they could. There was no cap for his head "but will have to do," Ever muttered to James while placing a horse blanket over the dead men they positioned together at the front of the bed. Ozzie did not want to know what his customers were doing, so he gingerly made his way back to his cubbyhole room to rest his tired body.

James drove Private Everson Golly and the dead Rebel privates to the basement prison entrance that Dolly had discovered. Ever told James to, "Wait here." In a blood-stained, stinking old gray uniform, Ever was able to enter the prison as Dolly had. Inside the damp and dark basement he made his way to rickety stairs that led him up to a door that was locked from the inside. He debated whether to knock and did so after the force of his shoulder failed to budge the oak door. Several times he knocked and waited…to no avail. When heading back down the rotted stairs –he heard a voice call out from behind the door. Ever ran back up the stairs and called out: "Burial detail! I need some help!" The door was soon opened by a white-haired old man in a butternut-faded uniform who pulled open the heavy door cautiously, demanding to know, "What's your business?" he drawled. Ever forced a smile and said, "I had to move my ambulance with two dead soldiers on it. I was sent here to get a

Yankee prisoner that just arrived here from Petersburg to dig the graves of these brave men." The old man hesitated…then called out to another guard nearby to: "Lock this here door behind me!"

The old guard followed Ever through the basement and outside to the ambulance where he saw the covered dead bodies and James at the reins.

"You got a nigger can dig those graves!" the old man pointed at James.

"He's free and won't dig unless he's paid. I can't force him to dig."

The old codger scowled at the big toothy smile James flashed him and muttered obscenities while walking toward the front entrance to the prison with Private Golly on his heels, agreeing with the old jailer. Right before entering the prison, Ever stopped the old man and in his quiet gentlemanly drawl he said, "I got a good look at the Yankee who shot those brave men in the back. After he digs their graves…he's gonna join 'em. My brigade would appreciate that, sir," Ever looked into the old man's green, rheumy eyes. The jailer asked Ever if he had a sidearm.

"Don't need one. I got a shovel," Ever said.

Ever followed the man into the prison; he passed armed sentries guarding ominous doors that the old man unlocked. They stepped into a vast room that held the huddled prisoners who were being admitted and registered by Rebels seated at a cluttered table. Ever was looking for Buck in this confused mass of Libby prisoners, these men in blue who were now standing on bare feet, their socks and footwear on the way to the Rebel trenches at Petersburg.

In the midst of his barefoot captive audience, as if in a camp of miners and prospectors, loquacious Bucklin Dunn was already using his business salesmanship savvy, convincing some of his fellow prisoners that he was neither a *"Billy Yankee nor Johnny Reb."*

"I came here on a clipper ship that left port in San Francisco, sailed clear around South America to Norfolk. I bought this here uniform in San Francisco so that I could reach my family in the Blue Ridge unencumbered by General Grant's siege."

Surrounded by Rebel guards brandishing an array of firearms, the new prisoners were unaware that they were being looked over by a red-headed Rebel who soon walked right into their ranks and grabbed the Yankee imposter from behind his neck with a powerful grip and from behind whispered something like: "Don't say a word." When Buck turned around, and before he could show any sign of surprise from seeing Everson in a blood-stained stinking Rebel uniform –he was literally dragged out of the holding area by his blue collar until he found himself outside and pushed toward the waiting ambulance and its familiar driver. From Libby's front entrance the old jailer watched the Yankee prisoner hop up into the ambulance with his Rebel escort and drive away. Meanwhile: the Yankee prisoners inside were explaining to their captors at gunpoint what the Yankee prisoner had been telling them –a story that didn't match what the old jailer told the Rebel guards.

On the moving ambulance bed, Ever told Buck to remove his Union shirt, which he did right away as they neared the hospital. Behind them, they could hear a man calling out to them to "Halt that ambulance!" Soon, the sound of gunfire caused James to duck down and speed up the horses. Buck and Ever could now see guards from the prison aiming at them with their weapons.

"Stay down!" Ever yelled to Buck and James as the Rebels pursued them on foot, then every so often a guard would stop to aim and fire at the ambulance.

A block away, James could see Confederate soldiers resting against a building, so he called back to Ever, "Which way?"

"To the river!" Ever yelled, causing James to whip the reins and turn right just past the livery.

Down the cobblestone street they rolled toward the river as Rebel lead began to whiz and zip all around them, one shot striking one of the ambulance horses on its flank, splattering blood onto James, who was leaning low on the buckboard as Buck and Ever used the dead men as shields against the incessant storm of lead striking and splintering the wagon's bed into wooden shards of shrapnel that struck the fleeing trio now and then. It was as if all of Richmond was firing at them until James turned right on River Road, giving them a brief respite from the firestorm of lead.

Soon, Rebels sharpshooters were firing at the wagon from rooftops, many positioned atop Libby Prison and the hospital. The brick road was rougher near the river with bricks missing or crumbled away; it was as if the wagon's wheels would fall off any second as Ever called up to James to head for the West Wharf, a long dock spanning nearly halfway across the James a couple blocks away. But then: both of the horses were shot dead, causing all of the human cargo to fly forward through the air and landing in a horrific crash a city block from the dock. James had landed face-first on one of the dead horses with such force that his jaw was broken; he struggled to breathe upon having his wind knocked out of him while Buck and Ever were bruised and scraped badly upon landing and skidding on the rough brick road. They both limped over to James, and together they all ran hunched over toward the dock as lead started pouring down from several downtown Richmond rooftops

Ever called out for Buck and James to stay spaced apart in order to diminish their target size. Buck was first to reach the dock, then James. Then: Ever was struck by a shot that went clean through his back and out his right chest area, tearing and collapsing his right lung. Face-down on the dock Ever waved for the boys to go on without him. No way were James and Buck going to leave Everson Golly, so both men stayed low and hustled back to their fallen leader, each one moving as fast as they could with Ever between them, his feet dragging along the wooden dock as lead whizzed by all around them. Gasping for air, Ever kept pleading for them to leave him.

It was a 10-foot drop from the end of the dock to the cold river that they made together, both James and Buck refusing to let go of an arm that belonged to the man they would never leave behind. Still between the boys in the water, each one holding an arm as they side-stroked with one arm in tandem against a current running east that made them a moving target and more difficult to hit as lead continued to miss them.

James was struggling emotionally: it was as if they were back in the shark-infested Atlantic swimming for The Dutchman. The images of that memory were shooting adrenaline to his brain as Buck did his best to stay with his brother's increased strength in the murky river. And Buck had his own reverie: recalling so many images of how Ever had rescued him and Dolly from certain death on The Dutchman. Soon, both young men were sobbing and shivering in the cold river, each one imploring Ever to keep his head above water as lead splashed close to them and whizzed past them in alarming frequency.

They kept on, beyond physical exhaustion, unsure of what or who would be on the other side of the river. All Buck and James could do was to keep stroking with one aching arm that would have to fall off before any one of them would stop. James and Buck forgot about their own injuries from the ambulance crash, both knowing that land was yet another hundred meters away as sharpshooters continued trying to pick them off from the rooftop of Libby Prison.

By the time they could touch bottom, Ever was pale blue and unconscious yet still breathing; he bled at the entry and exit wounds when they laid him on his side on the riverbank behind the trunk of a fallen oak tree. All three of them were now safe from the lead that continued overhead and struck the tree that protected them. James tore off his shirt and ripped it to pieces, securing it around Ever's upper torso to stop the bleeding from both wounds. Now, both James and his brother were exhausted and bareback; Buck was in bare feet as it neared sunset and the shooting had ceased. James and Buck agreed to wait awhile before moving, since it was too far to the tree line. Buck removed the wet derringer from his waistline pocket and left it on the tree to dry.

"Where'd you get that?" James asked his brother.

"An old Yankee vet I met in Grant's tunnel."

"You stay here with Ever while I get the wagon. It could take four or five hours to get back. It would take double that if we all go. Get in the woods after nightfall," James said.

Buck agreed with the plan, still shivering from the swim across the river.

"You say Virginia came home?" James asked his brother.

225

"Yes. She walked back on her own."

James was so relieved to hear that good news; it seemed to restore his energy. Soon, James crouched low and ran to the woods with no shots fired from across the river. Buck knew he had to get Ever into the trees in case there were Rebels in pursuit. Buck didn't think there would be anybody trying to find them, since Grant was keeping every available Rebel manning the trenches at Petersburg; and besides that –Buck was so tired from his swim he didn't want to try carrying Ever until he'd regained his strength. He removed his Yankee-blue pants to dry them in the breezes wafting across the river.

So there they were, huddled close together behind this fallen tree as night fell to the chirping cicadas all along the river's tree line behind them. Ever was shivering more now, causing Buck to press his body close to Ever's upper back to warm him.

"Take me home," Ever whispered.

"We will. James went for the wagon," Buck wept into the neck of the brave man who once again had risked his life for him.

Tell Me About Your Life

In dry Yankee trousers Buck managed to carry Ever over his shoulder into the woods where they now sat propped against a mound of dirt Buck had built up to support Ever in order to help his labored breathing. Buck could see in the moonlight the road James said he would use on his return to them in the wagon. Ever was conscious and shoulder-to-shoulder to Buck, who had several scrapes and contusions on his bare upper body and on the bottoms of his bare feet.

"I can't wait to get home and soak my body in the water," Buck whispered.

"Tell me about your life," Ever whispered above the hissing sound of escaping air coming from his covered chest wound.

Buck positioned himself against the mound on his side so he could talk softly into Ever's ear.

"It was all so incredible just getting there. I joined a wagon train of Mormons in Saint Louis and we went clean across to California, seeing the most incredible country, Ever. There were vast plains and always a mountain to cross. Didn't see a single Indian…except for a squaw and her baby having a bath in a stream where we camped. I got to Sacramento, California, and started right off selling canteens that I called *Bucklin Dunn* and even put my own stamp on each one. I'd go out all week just like we did in Richmond. Ever, I'd sell every canteen and go

227

back for more. I'd sell prospectors and miners and just about any man in need of a good canteen."

The fixed smile on Ever's face made Buck continue:

"I got rich, Ever; and I bought this land near the Russian River twenty miles from the Pacific Ocean. I'm gonna build a big house there for all of us to live in. I know I should've written you all to let you know how I was doin'. But I was afraid you'd want me to come back and I just couldn't stop sellin'."

Ever nodded that he understood and whispered, "Did you find your father?"

Buck turned his face away, his mouth faltering with emotion when he could say, "No. I never really cared about that. I figured…I found my father…on The Dutchman."

Ever had to ask Buck why he was wearing a Yankee uniform.

"I bought it in San Francisco. I kept hearin' how Grant was gonna take Richmond, so I thought I might need it to get around. I got caught up in Grant's tunnel, and before the big explosion they put me in with Burnside's Ninth Corps. Then they captured me."

Buck removed the hidden derringer the old Yankee vet gave him in the trench just before the assault after the explosion. He showed it to Ever, and told him, "I was gonna use it in the prison if I had to. It got wet in the river and I don't know if it'll even fire now." Just then: Ever's eyes closed, and Buck got scared until he saw his shallow breathing. Now and then over the next few hours the road came alive with the sounds of a rolling wagon, a rider on horseback, or pedestrians shuffling by on the

dirt road near them that was nothing more than a wide path
rutted from wagon tracks. It seemed to get harder for Buck to
hear the air escaping from Ever's wounds. Both Ever and Buck
had swallowed enough river water crossing the James, however
Ever was febrile and had been sweating it out since James had
left for the wagon. Twice during the night Buck made his way
back to the river to fill his mouth with water, enough to
eventually fill his hand to cover Ever's burning face and parched
lips.

***

By the time James showed up in the wagon it was sunrise.
Ever was unconscious, and once they put him onto the wagon's
bed he had to be stripped of his Rebel uniform because of the
Yankee's extended left flank between them and Lynchburg.
Once Ever was covered with a blanket made by Rebecca –they
had to turn around somewhere and head back west. Three times
on his trip back James had been stopped by Yankee sentries and
turned away. On his own he found a safe crossing of the
Appomattox River near Amelia Court House. This obscure route
would add several hours to their ride home at the very least.

James had managed to get water at the plantation when he
picked up the wagon. An old Golly Springs salt customer
recognized James and his wagon on the road and gave him a
bunch of green apples. Then: not long into the rough ride home
–Ever began coughing up blood and bleeding again from both
wounds. Buck had to elevate Ever's upper body by holding him
up at a sitting position with Ever between Buck's legs and
Buck's back braced against the bone-jarring buckboard. Ever
was barely able to sip water from Buck's palm, the spillage cold
to Ever's burning flesh on this journey home that already seemed
longer to Buck than his voyage around South America to
Norfolk.

Buck continued whispering to Ever about things he had seen while away: *"the bluest skies he'd ever seen were beyond the Rockies; the golden hills of California, where all men are free to pursue their dreams."* And he had to talk about the future, when *"Rebecca, Dolly and Virginia could buy the finest clothes on earth in the shops of San Francisco."*

It had taken more than three long hours to get around Grant's left flank; with at least a 12-hour ride ahead of them, Buck became dubious whether Ever could survive such a trip in his waning condition. Buck blamed himself for being in a position to get captured, causing this most horrific of circumstances.

***

Another sun was going down; James had kept his brown eyes on the Blue Ridge, praying that Ever could make it home, where Rebecca and the girls could attend to Ever after he'd soaked in the healing waters while he raced to Big Lick to fetch a doctor.

With most of their journey behind them –Buck could feel Ever's last breath leave his body. Grief and sadness overcame James and his brother as they pulled over and wept in each other's arms at the back of the wagon. The war had finally reached Golly Springs. The man who had raised three orphans was gone from the same rumbling wagon he had captained ten thousand trips to Richmond and back, across the war-torn sea of land in order to support his family.

Buck took the reins so James could have his time with Ever, this white man who had been a father to him and spared him the chains of slavery that few of his color managed to escape. Now and as many times before –James thanked God for sending

Everson Golly to him. He and his brother wept all the way home.

Reconstruction

Everson James Golly was born seven months after his grandfather was buried in the woods a few paces from the healing waters of Golly Springs. "E. J."'s parents, his Aunt Dolly, and Grandma Golly, continued living in their homes at Golly Springs for four years after Lee's surrender at Appomattox Court House, not far from the road where Ever had died on his way home.

Now: Bucklin Dunn, wearing the finest suit money could buy, stood on the pier of San Francisco Bay spotting the long-awaited steamer ship from Norfolk with a spyglass his company sold to mariners up and down the west coast. His buggy driver and two of his thirty *Bucklin Dunn* wagons awaited the arrival of the ship with their employer. Buck was thinking about how he set sail for San Francisco three months after Ever died, leaving it to his sister to convince them all to come to California with their belongings after their property was sold in Virginia. Dolly had waited until a few weeks after Everson James was born. Her words to James and Virginia tipped the scales toward California:

"You will have to wait too many years for these people to welcome you as equals. There will be many years of resistance after the war. You must get away from the pain these people will suffer long after the war is over. To give up their way of life will be hard for them; yet harder it will be giving up the cause their

*loved ones lost and gave so much for. You cannot expect E. J. to
wait for them."*

Uncle Buck had paid his family's moving expenses to make
this last voyage to California, to begin new lives together on the
land and homes he bought and built for them. At this minute,
three private rooms were waiting for them in the city's finest
hotel, where they would rest until James had his already-
scheduled and much-needed surgery done on his jaw that had not
set properly after his injury while escaping from Richmond. A
prominent San Francisco doctor told Buck he would be ready the
day James arrived at his office. This was a gift Buck wanted to
give his brother for taking care of the family while he attended to
his booming dry goods business *Bucklin Dunn & Company.*

Standing tall on the pier, looking through his spyglass he
was able to see his brother holding his nephew on the bow of the
steamer. Many times as well as this moment in his life since
leaving home, he had felt Ever's spirit all around him. In every
business dealing, Bucklin Dunn was admired for his strength and
energy, as well as his will to succeed. To many it was as if he
had the strength of two men. He did.

Standing at the ship's bow against the railing with his son in
his arms, brother James was the first to see the man with the fine
red hair in a suit waving at them from the wharf. It made him
hold his son closer to his chest; and, although his smile was
crooked now –the pain in his jaw abated with the thrill of
gratitude upon seeing his brother waiting for him, waiting in this
new world where they would be free to live their lives in peace.
Tears of joy streamed down the crooked face of this man who
would be a good father. He too would teach his son the only
word that mattered for every single thing that came his way, the
same word his adopted father taught him to feel every day of his
life: *"Gratitude." Without this word written on your heart,* Ever

would often say, *"comes anger and a life of accumulated resentments."*

As the steamer made its slow approach to land, the Golly women appeared from their private rooms. Prompted by the women, James laughed and cried with a joyous heart when he saw his son waving back at this stranger on the wharf, this red-headed man who brought them safely across the sea, to a new world they would never face alone.

THE END

"Writing a novel is like leaving a safe and worn path in order to take a route nobody has ever taken. It's dangerous and risky, and all for the hope of finding you, my reader."

www.michaelfrederick82.com